She Likes Sugar

Jo Dinage

Peltrovijan Publishing
P.O. Box 768
Greenbelt, MD 20768-0738

http://www.opeart.com

She Likes Sugar

PRINTING HISTORY
Peltrovijan Publishing/2021

ISBN: 978-1-937143-52-7
Printed in the United States of America

Inspired by my college years at UWI

She Likes Sugar

Jo Dinage

Other Published Works

Death of the Immortals

After a series of mysterious mishaps, a deep space explorer was forced to land on the unexplored planet of Alloca. Far from Mother Earth, the explorers were determined to survive on what they believed to be an uninhabited world. The Presidential Council decided to adopt a master policy. Through forced interracial marriages, they would create a single race of people.

Mind Games

Matthew has the uncanny ability to influence people's thought. To defend himself against the bullies, Matthew is eventually forced to use his special power.

The Starlight Kids, Mystery of the Feather Burglar

With the help of her friends, Shari gets her chance to turn a boring summer vacation into a fantastic action-packed adventure.

Linked

Same age, same height, same grade—they could have been identical twins, but they were not. Yet they lived in the same imperfect world with overwhelming family problems... One was black and the other was white and they had switched!

The Intruders– In This War They Had the Advantage

Six Bronx teens have one thing in common–a thirst for excitement! They get that and more when they set out to explore a neglected track of land in their neighborhood and embark on an adventure of a lifetime. Unfortunately, within weeks, their adventure becomes all too real as brother turns against brother, friends become enemies and people are being killed! This is no longer fun. This is war!

Life After High School: Traits that Help and Traits that Hurt
This no-nonsense text explains positive and negative traits that can help or hinder teens in their post high school life. The guide gives readers strategies, helping them to identify the path to success and to avoid the route that often leads to failure.

The Dangers of Medical Radiation
It is one of the ironies of medicine that radiation, as in x-rays, CT scans, radiation therapy and nuclear medicine can cause cancer yet can be used to detect and treat cancer. Perhaps because of this irony, most of us know very little about radiation dangers. Read how to protect yourself from medical radiation!

Chapter 1

Jamaica, West Indies early 1980s

Jen trailed silently behind her twin, head down. She kicked moodily at a stone in her path. Neither Josie, her twin, nor her twin's friend, Denise, found her behavior odd. Denise was half black, half East Indian and was Josie's best friend. They were accustomed to Jen's silence; besides, they were engrossed in their own conversation.

The girls were on their way to school, a mere fifteen minutes' walk from home. Although none of them noticed it, it was a lovely walk along the tree-lined avenues. The sun, cool at this hour, barely filtered through the trees, creating an intricate pattern of leaves on the ground.

Jen sighed. Sulking would achieve nothing, besides, unlike Josie, she rarely sulked for more than a day. And Josie, well aware of her twin's tendency, simply ignored her when she was sulking, knowing that she would soon come around. This morning was a prime example. When Jen got up early, had a glass of orange juice then disappeared into her room, Josie had assumed that Jen was sulking over something and had just ignored her.

What to do? Jen bit on her lips as she thought back on the scene of last night.

She had always felt that her aunt and uncle had created a pretty neat design for their home, especially considering that they were not architects. It was like a sandwich–with the verandah, living room, and dining room plus kitchen representing the 'filling' in the middle–then, on one side two bedrooms surrounded a bathroom, and on the other side, the bathroom was surrounded by the master bedroom and a study room cum library. Spoiling the sandwich effect was the washroom and a screened porch, which together and ran the entire length of the back of the house. However, Jen wasn't complaining because with three bedrooms each girl had a room of her own.

Last night Jen woke up feeling thirsty. After drinking a glass of water in the kitchen, she decided; since she was wide awake, she'd get the book she had been reading the day before.

I may as well finish it now, she thought, then I can change it at the school library tomorrow. She easily made her way, in the dark, to the opposite wing of the house. The study room was the first room on this wing and as she was about to enter, she absently noted the dim light peeping out from under the closed door of the master bedroom. It didn't quite register however, because she was so intent on getting her book. She began groping along the wall for the light switch.

She heard a giggle…

Jen's eyes widening in disbelief. She stood perfectly still, listening intently. Sure enough, the sound was repeated. Someone was giggling and the sounds were coming from their aunt's and uncle's room. There it was again! Could Uncle Jack have a woman in his room? Jen bit worriedly at her lips. Their Aunt Beryl was a nurse and usually worked nights. As far as Jen knew, her aunt had got up at her usual hour and had left for work. Could she have returned? There were more sounds coming from the room and, indistinct though they were, they definitely were the sounds of two people…doing…something. Jen began feeling hot with embarrassment. Forgetting her quest for the book, she abruptly went back into the living room. What should she do? She stopped in the short corridor between her room and Josie's. It was late but she simply had talk to someone about what she had heard. She started towards Josie's room, which was at the front of the house. Jen quietly opened the door, and hurried across the room, meaning to shake Josie awake.

"Josie...Josie," she called softly as she approached the bed.

She stopped. The room was dark, however, between the streetlight, filtering through the curtains, and the moonlight, there was sufficient illumination–sufficient for Jen to realize that the bed was empty.

She couldn't believe it! She went right up to the bed. Where was Josie? Had she gone partying with a friend? Josie had sneaked out before, but usually she told Jen. Jen was biting her lips as she went back to the door and switched on the overhead light. She looked around the empty room, not quite believing Josie wasn't there. She wasn't even sure what she was looking for or why she bothered to switch on the light, perhaps because she still could not believe that Josie not in her room. She switched off the light, quietly backed out of the room, and closed the door.

Jen paused at the dark and empty bathroom. Unconsciously, she had hoped that Josie had merely gone to the bathroom. She slowly entered her room, closed the door, and went over to her bed. She sat down. She wasn't sure just how long she sat there. Her thoughts were chaotic.

"What time is it anyway?" she wondered aloud,

turning to look at the luminous dials of the clock on her bed's headboard.

3 o'clock.

Could Josie be crazy enough to be at a party at this hour? There would be hell to pay if Aunt Beryl or Uncle Jack ever found out. This brought her thoughts back to her uncle. So worried had she been about her twin, she had forgotten her initial discovery. She pushed herself further up on the bed then sat hugging her knees and staring into space. An explanation had occurred to her, but she wasn't quite willing to face such a possibility as yet.

She was startled out of her reverie by a sound. It was Josie's room door opening–it squeaked slightly–a sound so slight she hadn't even noticed it before. She hugged her knees even tighter.

Josie had been in the house all along! Had she been returning from outside she would not have used that door. Her room had an entrance from the verandah, in front….

Jen suddenly looked up from her morose contemplation of the sidewalk. They were almost at school, and she still didn't know what to do. She wished there was someone she could confide in.

The minister? No. She didn't really know him. She didn't really know anyone, she realized suddenly. Her friends were really Josie's friends. Even Denise, whom they had known since starting at Gretagur High School, was Josie's best friend. She had never before felt a need for friends of her own and had simply relied on Josie's. Jen thought briefly of telling her aunt.

"I must talk to Josie first," she muttered, then realizing that she had spoken aloud, looked quickly at Josie and Denise. Neither had heard. Snatches of the conversation between them reached her.

".... The Chemistry teacher, you mean?" Josie was asking.

"No! Are you crazy? He is old," Denise laughed. "This guy is new. You must know him. He's tall and I think he is part Chinese. I don't know his name. But I love him already. I wish he was teaching us."

She means the new fifth form Physics teacher, Jen thought. She didn't say it aloud though. She still couldn't bring herself to speak to Josie. How could Josie? Could she have misinterpreted the whole thing? She sighed again and looked about. They had just turned on the school street.

Gretagur, their school, was in fact three separated, distinct, yet adjoining schools. There was the Preparatory school for girls and boys, aged three to twelve, then the Girl's High School and the Boy's High School for older children. Although the preparatory school was private, the High schools, like most other High schools in Jamaica, were government funded, and therefore free to all students who passed the Common Entrance Examination–the exams taken by all children at about age eleven.

Denise had attended Gretagur just about all her life, having started in the Preparatory school at age four. The twins however, had only started at Gretagur about eight years ago. They had transferred to Gretagur Preparatory School from the Primary school they had been attending. After one year at the Prep School, they sat and passed the Common Entrance Examination. Fortunately, both passed at the first sitting, and so were able to move on to the High school together. Gretagur was one of the best schools in Kingston–the capital of Jamaica–and Jen remembered that their parents, their mother in particular, had always wanted them to attend Gretagur. When their parents were alive however, money had always been a problem. Jen suspected that it was the insurance money that paid for their time at Gretagur Prep.

I can't go on like this, she decided. This was not the first time she had resolved to stop being Josie's shadow. Each time in the past, after a few days of trying, she had capitulated. She had convinced herself that there was no need to change since she wasn't hurting anyone. Beside it took a tremendous amount of effort to make a change and Josie often resisted her effort. In fact, Josie was the one who most objected to her changing. Now it was past time. She was determined to do something about her life, even if changing would upset Josie. Starting from today she vowed to stop following Josie around and relying on her twin for everything….

Their lives had been so different before their parents died. They were a normal happy family. They used to love dressing alike, making it difficult and sometimes impossible for strangers to tell them apart. It had been fun then to trick or even confuse others by pretending to be each other. That had all changed with the sudden death of their parents. Jen frowned as she instinctively shied away from thoughts of her parents. She still had much too vivid a memory of the accident.

Their father often took them to places of interest all over the island. We are "dry land tourist," was what he used to say teasingly, meaning they vacationed without leaving Jamaica–without, "crossing water" so to speak, since Jamaica was an island. So almost every year they went on a driving vacation, choosing a different location every time. That year they had decided on Ocho Rios, a beautiful town in the Parish of Saint Ann on the northern coast of the island.

They spent most of the day at the Dunn's River Falls, with its beautiful white sand beaches and waterfalls which fell 600 feet over a unique formation tier of rocks. Their mom didn't want to climb the falls and stayed on the beach, but both Jen and Josie climbed to the top with their dad. Although they followed the official guides and even wore the special slip-proof water shoes, the climb was still tricky in spots – especially because the water slick rocks were sometimes dangerously slippery.

They were tired but happy as they began the journey home. For Jen, the car drive was just an extension of the fun. She loved car trips and since they lived on the south coast, getting home meant a three-and-a-half-hour journey over the mountains, which ran like a spine down the center of the island. The main road was winding and narrow as it snaked up one side of the mountain and continued around hairpin turns and twists through a mountain pass. Yet the view was incredible, with a sheer drop on one side and the majestic mountain on the other. Her favorite area was located between Ocho Rios and Spanish Town, another small town. It was called Bog Walk gorge which is actually a corruption of the Spanish "Boca de Agua" meaning "Water's Mouth." The gorge was formed by the Rio Cobre River cutting a deep channel between towering rocks. The low bridge just skimmed the water and had no protective rails. Jen loved it! Her dad told her it bridge was often completed overrun by the river during the rainy season.

On the mountain road drivers depended on their horns to announce their presence but the loudness of the horn did not always translate to a large car or truck and Jen often made-up games guessing the size of an approaching car. If would be more fun if only Josie would get involved, but Josie's attitude to a car ride was just the opposite of Jen's. It was a standard joke in the family that the easiest way to get Josie to sleep was to take her for a ride in a car. This trip was no exception and while Josie slept, Jen was wide-awake. She marveled at the passing scenery…and sang….

"Brown girl in the ring, Tra la la la la, Brown girl in the ring, Tra la la la la."

Stop bouncing Jen dear," her mother called from the front seat of the car. "You'll rock the car and disturb daddy's driving."

"I'm not bouncing mommy." Jen gave a little bounce as she completed the next verse of the rhyme. "And she likes sugar, and I like plum …"

"Jen!" her mother warned.

Jen made a face. However, she did, reluctantly, stop bouncing on the seat as she repeated, "And she likes sugar and I like plum…"

"Mommy, Jen's singing is waking me up," Josie called out. "And she's singing it wrong. That's not how it goes," Josie was frowning at her twin.

"My singing didn't wake you," Jen protested. "I always sing, and you always sleep. And I want to sing it like this."

"Mommy, Jen is singing it wrong," Josie leaned forward to get her mother's attention. "That's not how the song goes."

Their mother turned to smile at Josie. "Why not sing it your way when Jen's finished her singing?"

"That's not fair!" Josie was not appeased. "You always take her side. Shut up, Jen!" She followed her demand with a forceful jab in her sister's side.

Jen immediately retaliated, her forceful push propelling her twin across the back seat.

"Ouch, that hurt!" Josie cried. "Daddy! Jen hit me!"

"Jen!" Her father called out sternly. He turned to take a quick look behind him but before he could comment further, Jen screamed.

"Daddy!"

Jen's eyes were focused on the road where a car ahead was inexplicable attempting to overtake. They were on a narrow two-lane road, with the mountain on one side, and a steep precipice on the other, there really was no room for error, and the overtaking car was now coming directly at them.

Unfortunately, Jen's father was startled by her scream. He jerked the wheel and the car swerved in the wrong direction— towards the precipice. There was a blare of horns as her father desperately attempted to make the correction. It was too late. Their car skidded wildly....

Jen screamed again. Hers was not the only scream. She heard the screams of both her mother and sister. That's the last thing she heard....their screams....

Her father had turned around to say something to *her*. That fact still haunted her. Perhaps he would have seen the oncoming car in time if he hadn't been distracted.

None of them had been wearing seatbelts and somehow, her door must have flown open, and she had been thrown clear of the wreck without serious injury. Her memory was a bit fuzzy after that. Maybe she was knocked unconscious for a while, but it couldn't have been for long because she remembered getting up and frantically trying to get back into the car. She even remembered calling to Josie…to her mother…to her father. There was blood everywhere. Josie was covered with it. Jen actually thought Josie was dead. She remembered the horror of seeing her father; remembered shouting at him to get up. He was bent over and since the door was gone, she tried to pull him out but stopped when she realized that his face was all squashed in and covered in blood. She vaguely remembered screaming, but nothing was clear after that.

She guessed other people must have arrived and helped because her next clear memory was of being in the hospital. Her Aunt Beryl had come to visit. She didn't question her aunt and her aunt didn't volunteer any information. She was released from the hospital after two days as she had suffered only a concussion. It was then she learned that Josie was still alive…. seriously injured but alive.

For weeks after she had lived in a daze, fearful of losing Josie too and uncertain of their future. During the three months that Josie spent in the hospital Jen had been barely alive; afraid of sleeping, because of recurrent nightmares; unwilling to talk; scarcely eating; and hating one song in particular. After trying for a while her aunt and uncle, busy with their own lives, had simply given up and left her to her spend her days mostly at Josie's bedside. No one forced her to attend school and it had been a relief for her and for them when Josie recovered.

Josie, who seemed to derive some comfort in "managing" her twin, took over completely. Initially, Jen's guilt overrode her common sense. She felt she had to make up for causing the accident so she didn't want to distressed Josie, and Josie would become extremely upset if Jen resisted or tried to express a differing opinion. Jen soon became reluctant to make her own decisions, often turning to Josie even before Josie interceded. The dependency rapidly escalated until Josie began answering questions addressed to Jen. Jen just wanted to keep Josie happy. Josie had never blamed her for the accident…yet it was there, perhaps subconsciously implied on Josie's part.

Jen could still remember her Aunt's explanation to others for her silence: "I'm afraid Jen has taken her parents' death rather badly," or "Please don't press her, she still hasn't got over her parents' death." Even Jen began believing that excuse. Her actions or rather, lack of action, kept the peace between her and Josie. By the time Jen started doubting the consequence of her passive behavior, everyone, herself included, had got accustomed to her silence and even accepted it. Over the years, she had made a few attempts to change. However, whenever she tried to express an opinion that differed from Josie's, Josie acted distraught…sometimes even crying and accusing Jen of hating her. The last time Jen refused to go with Josie to the beach, Josie had sulked for days. She had refused to talk to Jen. Which was why most times Jen's efforts to change were half-hearted at best and generally collapsed when Josie countered with a well-honed emotional push-back.

As they approached the school there were a lot more Gretagur girls on the road. The JOS bus pulled up before the school and spilled out twenty or so more students. JOS, the Jamaican Omnibus Service, was a company that everyone loved to hate. The buses were often crowded, and the service followed an unannounced, unadvertised schedule that was known to none.

"Hey! There is Sharon!" Denise pointed. She waved, then yelled, "Sharon! Wait!"

Sharon was a tall girl of East Indian origin. She turned around on hearing her name. Eyes narrowed against the sun, she scanned the area to locate the caller, finally smiling and waving as she spotted Denise and the twins.

"Come on Josie," Denise began urging Josie along.

The two increased their pace. Jen did not. Josie, realizing that her twin was not following slowed and turned around.

"What's the matter with you Jen?" She fumed. "Will you hurry up?"

"You go on," Jen called. She knew even without their stares that she had surprised them both. However, she had been Josie's shadow for eight years. It was time to stop.

"What in the world is wrong with you?" Josie asked. She was more puzzled than shocked, as yet unaware of the radical change Jen was going to make in her behavior patterns.

"Nothing." Since they had stopped, Jen was now only a few paces away. She shrugged, "Why don't you two catch up with Sharon and leave me."

Denise looked from on twin to another wondering what was going on.

Josie was clearly angry. She obviously felt that Jen was carrying a sulk too far. She grabbed Denise's arm, "Come on Denise."

"What's the matter with her?" Denise queried.

"I don't know, and I couldn't care less," Josie snapped.

Jen ignored Josie's final look of irritation. Josie was clearly baffled because sulk or no sulk, Jen always followed Josie.

The bell, marking the beginning of the school day, was sounding as Jen slipped in the classroom. There was a short silence, as everyone waited for some form of reaction from Josie.

Josie was at her desk. She had the hinged top cover open and looked busy sorting out her books for the day's lessons. The school was furnished with desks and chairs from another era. All the desks had attached chairs. The desk itself had a sunken compartment for books and a hinged cover. There was even an ink well which was no longer in use. All students were required to use fountain pens only, and in the past, the students had to manually fill the pen with ink from the ink well. Fortunately, they now had automatic refills.

"What's happened, Jen?" It was from Marcia, a tall slender girl with long blond hair, who usually sat in front of Jen.

Jen sat down and shrugged. She didn't feel up to answering any questions about her twin.

Denise answered. "They had a falling out. Jen walked off just as we got to school.

Jen wished she had the courage to tell her to shut up.

There were varying expressions of shocked, plain amusement and open curiosity on the faces of the other students.

She ignored all questions and after a while, the girls gave up, each little group resuming their previous discourse.

Josie however refused to even glance at her twin as Jen took her place at the desk besides her. She had obviously decided not to speak to Jen for the rest of the day.

It was a most unusual day for the twins. Since they had the same classes, all their teachers and classmates soon realized that they weren't speaking to each other. They would in fact have been surprised at the amount of discussion their dispute aroused. Mrs. Miller, their form teacher was the first teacher to become aware of the rift. She was duly informed by one of the students shortly after taking attendance—not directly of course. One of the girls allowed the information to slip out when Mrs. Miller failed to comment on the fact that Jen was not at Josie's side when they formed a line to go for morning devotion in the auditorium.

After devotion, Mrs. Miller passed on the information to other teachers in the staff room. There were a number of teachers sitting at their desks sorting out their days schedule or reviewing papers.

"Are you telling me Jen is no longer Josie's shadow?" asked Mr. Markland, the Physics teacher who Josie and Denise had been discussing on the walk to school. Although new at the school, he was already familiar with the twin's unusual habits.

"It seems so. I am not sure of the story behind the change, however."

"It is about time," Miss. Anderson, the Math's teacher, commented on hearing.

"I know what you mean," Mrs. Miller agreed. "I've tried on numerous occasions to at least get Jen to make a few decisions on her own. She is much too dependent on

Josie."

"You are right," another teacher spoke up, "They should have been separated years ago."

"Have you ever tried talking to the parents," Mr. Markland asked.

"Their parents are dead I believe," Mrs. Miller looked questioning at Mrs. Parks, the twins previous form teacher.

"Yes. They live with an aunt and uncle from what I can gather, and I have spoken to the aunt. She doesn't believe there is anything wrong with Jen's behavior."

"Or doesn't want to believe," Mr. Markland said. He crossed his legs, resting his right ankle on his left knee, and settled back in his chair. "I'm all for dressing twins alike–when they are babies–but at this age.... How old are they? Seventeen? Eighteen...?" he shrugged. "They should be separate people. They shouldn't even be attending the same school."

"Well in all fairness," Mrs. Miller put in, "They don't look alike even though they wear the same uniform. Jen styles her hair differently, and they certainly don't act alike. In fact, I would say Jen deliberate tries not to look like her twin."

Mrs. Parks was nodding. I believe the reason is, she doesn't want to be mistaken for Josie. She wants to fade into the woodwork as it is. The last thing she wants is to be noticed and forced to converse or participate in anything on her own, and that is what would happen is strangers kept confusing the two them."

"You are right," Miss Miller agreed. "It is not the fact that they are identical twins that is the problem. It is Jen's personality on a whole."

"Well, here we have an excellent opportunity to try to change all of that," Miss. Anderson said smiling. She gathered up her papers for the day. "I think I know how to give Jen a chance to find herself."

"How?" someone else asked.

"I'm going to try and get her on the Math quiz team. The challenge will be good for her. The interschool competition is due to start in a few weeks. I think she should be able to pass qualifying tests."

"Well, all I can say is, I wish you luck," Mr. Markland said pessimistically.

Miss Anderson merely smiled as she left the room. She was not discouraged by the general lack of support from the other teachers.

She was as good as her word. After the Math's lesson, Miss Anderson called Jen. "Could I have a few words with you Jen? Do you have a free period after this?"

"No Miss. Anderson, I've got Physics," as Jen approached the desk, she prayed she wasn't going to be grilled on her breakup with Josie.

"Oh! Humm, when do you have a break?"

Jen hesitated, what in the world could Miss. Anderson possibly want to talk to her about. Bending her head, she muttered, "In fourth period, right after lunch."

"Fine," Miss. Anderson smiled, after checking her schedule. "Meet me in the staff room then. And bye-the-way," she added when Jen did not look up. "Your problem with your sister is a personal matter between you and her. I don't intend to force any confidences," she paused, "Although I am available if you feel a need to talk to someone about it.

"Oh!" Jen looked up, startled. She then smiled

shyly, grateful that Miss Anderson had correctly gauged her feeling.

Jen walked off feeling less heavy hearted about things. She really didn't care that her classmates, taking their cue from Josie, were basically ignoring her. A shy and introspective person by nature, she did not mind being by herself. It was because she didn't mind being ignored that she had become virtually Josie's shadow. She recognized now that following Josie was taking the easy way. Josie did all the talking, made all the decisions.

When with Josie, both Josie and her friends would simply ignore her, even when she tried to participate in the conversation. She now realized that she had been trying to exert her own personality in the wrong way. The only way for her was to go it alone. Josie's friends could not automatically become her friends. She had to find her own way and make her own friends. Maybe that was what she had unconsciously realized and had been afraid to do, knowing how much her actions would upset Josie. She had just drifted along because she knew that making the break would be hard. She biggest fear was hurting Josie. Maybe she would sit down with Josie and try to explain everything.

She couldn't continue as before. She just couldn't. The scene last night, and her total distaste for what she felt had happened had finally given her the courage to do what she should have done a long time ago.

Later Jen left the staff room feeling quite pleased. Miss. Anderson wanted her on the Math's quiz team. She had never even thought of taking the test, since Josie wasn't interested. She had managed not to mumble her replies and more than once had expanded instead a giving a simple yes or no answer. It sounded like a simple accomplishment but for her it was a lot, and she was fighting to keep a silly grin off her face as she walked back to her Homeroom.

It wasn't far. The staff rooms and principal's office were located near the main entrance to the school, on one of the numerous tree-lined pathways that crisscrossed the grounds. The school itself has managed to retain a remarkable countrified air, considering that it was situated in the middle of a bustling city. The newer sections were the lower school, forms one through three. These building had a modern look with updated classrooms. The older sections included the three forms of the upper school, all the administrative buildings, the library, and the auditorium. This section was built over a hundred years ago when the school first opened. The few new buildings had been skillfully designed to blend in. Classes for most of the upper forms were conducted in small single-story buildings that looked like little cottages. Girls starting out at Gretagur generally thought the effect cute, that is, until they reached fourth form and began classes in one of the cottages. It was then they realized that since each cottage had only about four classrooms, changing classes usually meant taking a walk to another cottage. This was fine when the weather was sunny, but, during the rainy season, even a short walk could mean a drenching unless you were adequately covered.

Once back in her homeroom, Jen was sorting her books, in preparation for Biology class when Marcia approached.

"Did you finish all your Bio homework?" she asked.

Jen nodded, then, remembering her new resolution said aloud, "Yes." She gave a tentative smile as she gathered up her books and started for the door.

Marcia followed.

"Did you and Josie have a fight or something," Marcia asked.

Jen sighed inwardly. So, it's information she wants, she thought. She shrugged, and continued walking, not bothering to answer. She knew that she was reverting to what she had hoped was her habits of the past, but she couldn't help it. She didn't want to answer Marcia's question and this for her was the easiest, and most tried method of discouraging a questioner.

"Huh!" Marcia said rudely. "You're going to have to learn to talk now that Josie has abandoned you."

On getting no reaction to the insult, Marcia walked off in a huff.

During the course of the afternoon another student approached Jen, trying to find out the reason behind the break-up between her and Josie. Jen guessed Josie must have told them to get lost, which was why she was being harassed. She treated all but the last one in the same manner: she ignored all questions she didn't want to answer. She soon realized though, that her old method simply wasn't going to work. She was being called, "dumb," "stupid," and other assortment of derogatory terms. It seemed that Marcia was right, without Josie to answer for her; she would have to speak for herself!

She was on her way to the bathroom on leaving Art, the last class for the day, when she met Michelle. Michelle, a tall black girl with large almond shaped eyes, was very smart but friend-less, because of a seriously annoying personality trait.

Ever since coming to Gretagur a year ago, Michelle

has been boasting about her life, her parents; anything! Her parents had money, lots of money, and Michelle liked to make others aware of that fact. She also seemed to feel that she was better than everyone else and resented not been treated accordingly. The two girls almost bumped into each other. It was Jen's fault. She was walking with her head down, as was usual.

"Sorry," she muttered, attempting to pass Michelle.

"Oh! Jen...! It's you. That's all right," Michelle flicked her straight shoulder length black hair away from her face. She then reached out, grabbing hold of Jen's arm. The move was effective. Jen was unable to pass. "What did you and Josie quarrel about," she demanded, coming directly to the point.

"Nothing," Jen replied. Since Michelle had loosened her hold on her arm Jen began walking away.

"Hey! Wait a minute. I'm talking to you," Michelle tried to hold on to her again.

Jen executed a sharp body twist to avoid Michelle's grasp, "But I'm not talking to you."

She left Michelle staring after her in open-mouthed astonishment.

Jen's sense of exhilaration was indescribable, and to keep the mood she took a longer and more leisurely walk home after school. Besides, she wanted to avoid walking behind Josie who was with a group of her friends.

Her Aunt Beryl met her at the door.

"Why are you both so late? Aunt Beryl asked, then on looking around and behind Jen added "Where is Josie?"

"I think she stopped off with some friends of hers," Jen guessed. She had expected Josie to arrive before her. "Is Uncle Jack here?" she added.

Aunt Beryl stared at her, puzzled at the seemingly

irrelevant question. "You know that your uncle doesn't get in so early, and what do you mean, you think that your twin stopped off with some friends?"

Jen lowered her head. She wondered briefly if she could get away with a muttered comment then decided against it. She cleared her throat and began what turned out to be confused and jumbled explanation. "She left school with some friends. She was ahead of me. She was walking with her friends. Maybe she stopped. At least I think she did. I thought she would be home before me but now I don't know why because I didn't walk home with her."

Aunt Beryl sighed impatiently. "You left Josie with some friends you said?"

"Well... I don't know where she is," Jen admitted. "We didn't walk home together."

"You didn't...," Aunt Beryl stopped. "Don't try my patience Jen. You just told me Josie stopped off with some friends."

"Well.... I guess she did," began Jen, then hurriedly continued on noting her Aunt's angry stare. "You see, we didn't leave school together. Josie left first so I guess she must have stopped off with some friends since she isn't here."

"I...see," Aunt Beryl dragged out, clearly not 'seeing' at all. "Well....," she paused, then decided against saying anything. "Well," she started again, "I've started dinner, just carry on." Turning towards her room she continued, "Make sure you check that everything is properly cooked before you turn anything off and don't let anything burn. I'm going to get some more rest before getting up. You can all eat when your uncle gets in and don't bother waking me up. Okay, dear?"

"Yes, Aunt Beryl," Jen was glad there were no more questions. "I'll just go and change."

She was in the bathroom when Josie came in. Jen continued washing her hands, reluctant to face Josie. Finally, unable to delay any longer she turned off the tap and came out. Josie was about to enter her room. She ignored Jen completely, slamming her room door as she went in.

Jen hesitated. She had to speak to Josie sometime soon. She stood indecisively biting her lips. Finally, putting off what she knew would be an unpleasant interview, she went into the kitchen. After checking on the diner, Jen got her books and sat at the dining table to do her homework. She was afraid that if she moved to the study room, she would forget the food cooking. Half hour later she threw down her pen in disgust. She was getting nowhere. She simply couldn't concentrate on schoolwork. Her mind kept wandering to Josie and Uncle Jack and what she was sure she had heard. I must talk to Josie, she thought as she got up.

"If I think about it too much, I'll probably change my mind," she muttered aloud as she walked determinedly to her twin's room. She knocked on the door.

No answer.

Jen knocked again. "Josie, I need to talk to you."

No answer.

Jen bit her lips. Should she force a confrontation or should she forget the whole thing. No..., no.... She couldn't just forget what she had heard.

"Josie...? Josie...? It's about last night."

Still no answer.

Jen hesitated, then rapped softly. "Josie, I know about you and Uncle Jack," she whispered.

Silence.

"Josie?"

"Get lost, Jen," Josie made no effort to soften the harshness of her reply.

"Josie I must talk to you".

"What do you mean, me and Uncle Jack," Josie finally called back.

Her voice sounded distinctly aggressive. Jen's heart sank, despite what she had heard, despite what her rational mind indicated was obvious, she had been hoping.

"Can I come in," she now asked, "I don't want to keep shouting through the door."

"Okay," Josie responded grudgingly.

Relieved, Jen opened the door and stepped in. She then leaned against the closed door. Josie was sitting cross-legged on her bed. She had been reading a magazine and had bunched up her pillows behind her, using them as a back support.

"Well," she demanded challengingly.

Jen, after a quick glance at her twin's face, kept her eyes on the floor. "When I got up for a book last night, I heard you in Uncle Jack's room." She looked up to gauge her twin's reaction. Josie was pleating and re-pleating a fold in her skirt. Jen could tell that she was embarrassed.

"Josie, how could you?" she agonized.

"He loves me!" Josie instantly flared up. She jumped off the bed, folded her arms in front of the body and glared angrily at her twin. "Don't look at me like that. What do you know about love?" she waved a scornful hand in Jen's direction. "Just look at you. You are just like a zombie. Don't you come judging me. Jack says you are passionless. That's why no one likes you and you haven't got any friends... you don't even have a boyfriend. You're probably just jealous," she concluded spitefully.

Unbelievable hurt by the sudden attack, Jen stared at her twin. "If everyone liked you so much you would be able to find your own boyfriend, instead of stealing Aunt Beryl's husband," she retorted.

"I didn't steal him," Josie shouted.

"Keep your voice down! You'll wake Aunt Beryl," Jen stormed back.

"I didn't steal him," Josie repeated in a lowered tone, "He loves me, and I love him. Aunt Beryl doesn't love him; he used to practically beg her to sleep with him. Besides, he is going to divorce her and marry me as soon as I finish school. He just doesn't want to cause her any problems now, since we can't get married yet in any case." She paused for breath.

Jen stared at her twin in disbelief. Could Josie be that stupid? She was obviously repeating what she had been told. At the back of her mind, she knew that Uncle Jack was to be blamed for the affair, after all he was a grown man, yet she still felt that Josie could have refused him. She was disappointed in her twin, and there was Aunt Beryl to consider. She really should know. This whole thing just was not right. How could Josie?

"But he's still married to Aunt Beryl!"

For a minute, Josie looked discomforted. She shrugged and again resorted to what Jen was convinced was a rehash of Uncle Jack's justification. "Well, I don't like it, but he can't just–not be with her. She would want to know why."

"Aunt Beryl should know," Jen insisted. "He probably hasn't told her he doesn't love her and it's not fair to her. She is just being used."

"Since it hasn't hurt her this past year not knowing, it doesn't make any sense to tell her now."

"You mean this was not the first time?" Now Jen was truly horrified.

Josie had the grace to look shame faced.

"Oh Josie!... How could you?"

"Will you stop saying that," Josie snapped.

"Well, it's not right Josie. You know that it's not right. No matter how much he says he might love you, or you love him."

"Look Jen," Josie had calmed down, "As soon as we take our finals Jack will ask Aunt Beryl for a divorce. After a bit, he and I will get married. Aunt Beryl need never know that he loved me while still married to her. If we tell her now, she will be terribly hurt."

The argument made sense, in a way, although Jen still didn't like it. "It takes years to get a divorce," she protested.

"Jack knows someone who can speed it up." At Jen skeptical look she added earnestly, "Seriously Jen, he knows a lot of important people. He says that he can arrange everything in three maybe four months."

It didn't sound possible to Jen, but she wasn't knowledgeable enough to debate the issue. "Okay, I won't say anything to Aunt Beryl if the two of you stop... well stop...," she waved her hands vaguely in embarrassment.

"Really Jen," Josie looked pityingly at her. "Don't you know anything about men?" she asked rhetorically. She gave a superior smile. "I don't want Jack turning to some strange woman just because I refuse him. That's likely what happened in Aunt Beryl's case."

Jen felt her face getting hot. She was almost

positive that Josie was again simple spouting out Uncle Jack's justifications. However, she was too embarrassed to argue the point. Besides Josie was right, she didn't know anything about men. Refusing to meet her twin's eye she started backing out of the room. "Well...well...I'd better check the diner."

Josie laughed. "Grow up Jen. Sometimes I can't believe that we are sisters, much less twins. You don't know anything."

Jen fled.

Instead of going into the kitchen, she went into her room. Hugging herself she walked absently about the room. She hadn't solved anything. Josie knew that she wouldn't tell, which meant that Josie and Uncle Jack were going to carry on as before. She stopped in front of the mirror of the wardrobe and started frowning at herself. Was Josie right? Was she as passionless as Uncle Jack suggested? She had never really thought of having a boyfriend, or of having a girlfriend for that matter. She had been quite comfortable with her life before today. Josie took care of everything, and she just followed Josie along. How pitiful was that? Josie was right. She was a zombie. Should she try to change? The question was, how?

She cringed at the thought of being outspoken, like Josie. But maybe she could change her appearance? Jen began a critical assessment of features. There was nothing wrong with her looks, after all, she was Josie's identical twin and Josie was considered attractive. It was simply the way she dressed and styled her hair. A few years ago, Josie had talked her into treating her hair with a permanent cream. But, whereas Josie, Denise, Sharon and the other girls that Josie hung out with usually used rollers at nights so had a profusion of shoulder length curls in the mornings,

Jen simple couldn't be bothered and generally sported a ponytail.

Jen moved back to the edge of the bed sat and rested her elbows on her knees, chin in her cupped palms. She tried visualizing herself with curls. No…. It would never work! She didn't even like curls!

Jen took some deep breaths as she tried to figure out why she was so scared of the idea of changing her appearance. She didn't want to be popular! And in the background, just waiting to surface, a few beats of the song hovered, *'And she likes sugar, and I like…'* She squashed it ruthlessly. She was not going there. Focus, Jen….focus… She took another deep breath in, held it, then released her breath with a gasp, breathing deeply and sucking in air. The near oxygen deprivation and her effort to breathe took her mind from the events in her past. Jen went back to the mirror.

She didn't think it was just her hair and dress. After all, they wore the same uniform to school, and there were other girls at school who were popular and didn't have curls in their hair. If popularity were based solely on looks, half – if not more – of the students of Gretagur would be unpopular. Her thoughts shifted to Cecilia, a girl in their Arts class. She was wildly popular. Yet her hair was short, and she usually kept it in a natural style. Josie couldn't stand her, and she and Josie were always arguing about "Natural Black Beauty," whatever that was supposed to mean. It certainly meant something different to both of them, with Cecilia generally insisting that Josie was trying to look "white" by putting chemicals in her hair. Josie usually fought back by arguing that most women, black or white, treated their hair one way or another and that it was normal for a woman to try to improve her looks.

Jen didn't like Cecilia and generally tried to avoid her, not because of her hair but because Cecilia was proud of her cutting remarks, some of which could be extremely spiteful. Jen wasn't sure how her friends tolerated being snapped at on a regular basis. Even so, Jen had once tried to inject her point into an argument but had been totally ignored. She sighed. This really was depressing. That was basically her problem. She was usually ignored. To get a boyfriend or any friend for that matter she would need to change her personality. The problem is she was not sure she wanted to be noticed! She was not looking for a radical change in personality. She just needed to be more independent of Josie. She sighed again, then suddenly sat upright, tilted her head slightly, and listened. She had heard the front door opening. Uncle Jack was home! She would never be able to face him at dinner. She wondered if Josie would tell him that she knew about them.

"I'll ask Josie not to," she murmured to herself. She got up but hesitated as she heard Josie leaving her room. She listened to the indistinct murmur of voices, wondering what to do now. Then she heard her name.

"Jen!" Josie called again.

"Yes?" What did Josie want? She simply could face Uncle Jack just now.

"I thought you went to check on the dinner?" Josie asked opening her room door. She looked at her twin in annoyance. "You made just about everything burn. Can't you smell it?" She opened the door wider as if inviting in the smell.

"Oh!" Jen covered her mouth with her hand, "I forgot."

Josie made an exasperated noise. "Well, what's left

of diner is all set and Jack says he is ready to eat now."

Jen half turned away. She fiddled nervously with some books on her bed. "Did...did you tell him?" she asked.

Josie shrugged, "It doesn't make any sense to tell him. He would only be embarrassed."

Him and me both, Jen thought in relief. She gave her twin a tentative smile. "Both of you can go and eat. I'm not really hungry right now. I'll probably get something later. Okay."

Josie shrugged again. "Suit yourself," she said as she disappeared out the door.

The rest of the evening was uneventful. Although she was hungry, Jen remained in her room. Whatever explanation Josie gave for Jen's absence at the dinner table obviously satisfied Uncle Jack since he did not disturb her. Jen knew that she would have to face him sometime. After all, the three of them usually had breakfast and dinner together. She also knew that finding out about Josie's relationship with Uncle Jack would cause an irrevocable change in her relationship with her twin. She was no longer troubled about upsetting Josie. Although she was not yet sure if it would be for good or for bad, she was glad to be free of that particular burden. The course of her life would change!

Chapter 2

Over the next week and a half, Jen tried to forget the ongoing relationship between Josie and their Uncle Jack. She had tried once more to talk to her twin, but Josie was mad that Jen refused to condone her behavior. Josie felt that Jen was trying to make her choose and give up Uncle Jack. And unfortunately, Jen's refusal to condone Josie's behavior only seemed to reinforce Josie's obstinacy. Josie was now refusing to speak to Jen.

Jen decided to avoid both her aunt and uncle as much as possible. She felt embarrassed and uncomfortable in approaching either of them. Typically, she and Josie fixed breakfast and she would sit with Josie and Uncle Jack for breakfast and dinner. She began grabbing a fruit or snack and having it for breakfast in her room and waiting until much later when her Aunt Beryl got up in the evening to have dinner. Usually around that time Uncle Jack would leave the living room and head back to his bedroom. She also felt extremely guilty about hiding her knowledge from her aunt. The only good to come from the whole affair, was that she was no longer Josie's shadow. At home, more focus was placed on that, rather than on her unusual behavior towards her aunt and uncle, which was generally overlooked. Aunt Beryl tried once to find out what had caused the change. Jen simply said she thought that it was time that she led her own life and not Josie's. Her aunt, while not satisfied, agreed and left it at that.

Jen got the feeling that Aunt Beryl although

curious, was not overly interested in her reasons. But then, that was Aunt Berry. She was never very interested in them. Jen wondered whether her aunt had tackled Josie too. She had no way of knowing since she and Josie were now exchanging only the essentials when it came to words.

Jen believed her twin was being stupid. She didn't even like Uncle Jack and couldn't understand how Josie could possibly love him. What they were doing was also wrong, completely wrong. It was unfair to her aunt as well. She basically couldn't see how Josie could put up with Uncle Jack. He was using both Josie and her aunt. That was how she saw it, and while she was bitterly disappointed in her twin, she hated Uncle Jack for what he was doing. She wondered whether, Josie would have even started the affair with Uncle Jack if they had a closer relationship with their aunt.

It was a moot thought, however. Conversations between aunt and nieces were never intense. They rarely discussed anything beyond household chores and usually those were a variety of questions and answers. Looking back, she could not even remember being asked about schoolwork and Aunt Beryl rarely invited confidences. Jen remembered her first period. She had been bleeding for two days before she worked up the courage to tell her Aunt. She hadn't even thought to tell Josie. After two days of nightmarish worries about death and dying from a weird disease she received a matter-of-fact explanation for the unusual blood flow from her Aunt. She had quickly passed the information along to Josie who fortunately started her first period a week later. Jen had turned to the library and books for more information about her body. She vowed never to put any daughter through her experience and couldn't imagine why her Aunt didn't at least warn her. Then again, maybe her aunt didn't expect that she would keep the bleeding secret for two days.

She sighed. Aunt Beryl was just not child friendly. After their parent's death, being their only close relative, she had automatically taken them in. Jen had never before wondered if she had really wanted to. Thinking about it now, she realized that their aunt probably considered them a necessary duty. She provided for them; they were well dressed; they went to good schools. That was about it.

One of things that helped Jen to focus less on her problems was the plans, already underway, for a class Walk-a-ton. It was to be the upper six's final fund-raising event. Like most schools in Jamaica, their school usually conducted various fund-raising events to help with capital improvement, and, or social programs. The previous month, the fifth formers had decided to host a play. So far it was a huge success. They had sold tickets to both students, parents and outsiders, and the play was still running. Not to be outdone, the sixth formers had decided on a Walk-a-ton. There was no way you could lose money on a Walk-a-ton. There were no expenses so all monies collected would be profit. For this Walk-a-ton, the students planned to hike to Hollywell, a town fifteen miles up, in the mountains above Kingston. The students could collect as many pledges or actual monies as they could before the start of the Walk-a-ton. For example, a fellow student may pledge to pay the hiker two dollars per mile walked. This meant that for the thirty miles round trip walk, the hiker would collect sixty dollars.

In past years, Jen had depended entirely on Josie to solicit and collect for her. This year she intended to strike out on her own.

She focused on the lower school–third form and below–and began spending her free periods canvassing the girls there. Most didn't really know the twins and therefore were not aware that she was doing anything strange in moving about on her own. Accordingly, there were no questions and no strange looks, the two current plagues in her life. To her surprise, most students were willing to donate, even if not generously.

Jen was also finally able to call someone, 'friend.'

She had been studying for the Math's quiz–she had been doing lots of studies lately as studying helped her forget, at least for a time, her guilty feelings over her twin's and uncle's relationship. She had years of practice studying by herself since Josie had never been big on studying. In study sessions with Josie, she was often the one asking Josie the questions. Reviewing her notes by asking herself questions helped her to focus and asking Josie questions seemed to have helped Josie in the past. At school she soon found it best to find an empty classroom if she planned on studying. She didn't like going to the library–sitting by herself when there were so many cliques of students was no fun. She would get extremely self-conscious thinking that the other students were talking about her. She was therefore engrossed in her books, and by herself in an otherwise empty classroom one Monday, when Rita came in the room. Jen knew her slightly; she was in 'Commercial Six' since she was taking the secretarial courses available to students in that track. Rita was half-a-head shorter than Jen and almost always had her hair in braids. Since Jen was sitting in the back of the room, Rita was halfway in before she noted Jen.

"Oh!" she said, "I... I'm sorry. I...I didn't know there was going to be a class here this period." She started to leave.

"There's not. I mean there is no class here. I'm just studying for the Math's... well the Math's quiz."

"You... you're going to try out for the team?" Rita stared wide eyed.

Jen shrugged, "Well hopefully."

"Lucky you," Rita looked depressed. She came further in the room and plunked her books down on a desk close to Jen. "That's my worse subject. I'm just coming from an Arithmetic test–mind you Arithmetic, nothing complicated–which I just know I failed." She sank down in a chair and rested her chin in cupped palms.

"I'll help you if you like," Jen offered.

"You... really?" Rita raised her chin, staring.

"Well, sure," was Jen's immediate response.

"It probably won't make any difference," Rita cupped her chin again, and sighed, obviously deciding that it was too soon to drop her gloominess. "My teacher has given up. I believe even my Mom has given up. My brother certainly has. He says I am hopeless at even simple addition and subtraction much less Arithmetic, as if it's not the same thing."

"It can't be that bad," Jen was uncertain how to deal with what she suspected–but was not sure–was an exaggerated gloominess. "Maybe we could go over your problems."

Rita studied her. "Are you serious?" she asked, dropping her hands from her chin.

Jen nodded.

"What about your studies?"

"It can only help, after all it's Math isn't it. We can even start now."

They spent the rest of the period doing problems and gossiping, or rather Rita did most of the gossiping. Jen mostly listened. Not once did Rita question Jen about Josie, for which Jen was grateful, though curious as to whether it was thoughtfulness on Rita's part or merely that Rita loved talking about her family too much to focus on anything about others. Jen learned that Rita lived with her mother and older brother. No father was mentioned, and Jen did not feel it polite to ask. Rita's Mom worked as a secretary at the Ministry of Health in the town of New Kingston. Her brother worked in a lawyer's office in downtown Kingston. Jen gathered that he had left school about five years ago and had since got a degree in Accounting from the UWI, the University of the West Indies. Although working, he was trying to figure out how to further his studies. He was interested in law. From her tone when speaking about him Jen could see that Rita greatly admired her brother.

They were in the middle of their third problem when the bell rang.

"Gee! It's the end of period already?" Rita looked up in surprise.

"It looks like," Jen said glancing at her watch. She began packing up her books.

Rita did the same. "Thanks so much…for helping me," she gave Jen a big engaging grin.

"That's Okay," Jen shrugged to hide her delight. Someone appreciated her! "I enjoyed it." She then looked down, fiddling with her books. "If you like we could meet again. I mean…," she allowed her voice to trail off as she looked up, anxious to gauge Rita's reaction.

Rita was full of enthusiasm. She nodded eagerly, "When are you free next?"

They sat down to coordinate their free periods.

"Okay," Jen finally said, "We can meet on Mondays for the sixth period and on Thursdays for the third period." She frowned over her schedule of classes. "Pity it couldn't be Wednesdays instead."

"Why? Do you have something else to do on Thursday?" Rita questioned.

"Not really. But remember I am hoping to get on the quiz team?" At Rita's nod she continued. "Well, they usually have the interschool quizzes on Thursday."

"Oh! So, you would want the free period on Thursdays to study," Rita inserted.

"Maybe," Jen gave a little laugh. "Let's leave it at that. I'm not even on the team yet."

"Okay," Rita said. "If anything, we can always change it to once a week."

"All right. See you Thursday then." Jen took a quick glance at her watch. "I'm going to be late if I don't hurry. Bye."

Soon it was their routine. Jen and Rita would spend at least two periods a week studying together. Most of the time they met in an empty classroom, and they had the room all to themselves. Now and again, however, other students or groups of students used the room at the same time. On such occasions, if the other students were too noisy, they would simply go to the library, or if the weather was fine, sit on one of the benches under the trees outside. They were busy doing a problem in a classroom one day when Monique entered the room.

Monique was in Jen's form. She was a striking girl, tall with long blond hair. Jen was surprised to see her by herself however as she usually went around with two other students, Marcia and Kim.

"Oh!" she said on spotting them. "I thought the room was empty."

"Don't mind us," Rita said looking up, "We don't own the room besides there's lots of space."

Monique stood uncertainly at the door.

"Are Marcia and Kim coming?" Jen asked, wondering at Monique's uncertainty.

"No," Monique was abrupt.

End of conversation, Jen thought. She couldn't think of a single other thing to say, and she fully expected Monique to leave. She was surprised therefore when Monique asked.

"What are you two studying?"

"Math, lovely Math," Rita moaned.

Monique gave her a strained smile.

Rita, realizing that Monique was genuinely upset about something, began talking casually about the problem they were working on.

Monique joined them. She sat down on the seat next to Jen and seemed to be listening. She didn't talk however, nor did she make any effort to get involved with the actual working out of the problem.

Finally finished, Rita sat back and stretched. "Two down one to go," she said.

"How many do you usually do?" Monique asked. It was her first effort to actively participate.

"However, many we like, really," Rita turned to Jen, "Do you want to do another one Jen?"

Jen checked her watch. "We may have time for one more."

"She is a real slave driver," Rita said teasingly to Monique. She and Monique grinned as Jen ignored them and began looking through the textbook for another problem. As usual Rita began talking about her family.

"Your mother sounds nice," Monique commented, a touch of envy in her voice.

Rita stared at her in surprised, not knowing quite how to respond to such a remark. She finally got out, "I'm fortunate I guess."

"You don't know how much," Jen said. "You can ask your mother about anything...I mean you can discuss anything with her."

Monique nodded agreeing. "I know what you mean," she turned to Jen. "You can't talk to your mother either, eh."

"My aunt," Jen said. "My parents are dead."

"Oh! I'm sorry," Monique said.

"I didn't know that," Rita added.

Jen shrugged, "It was a long time ago when we...I was nine."

That must have been hard though," Rita looked concerned. "I mean, you probably still miss them, right?"

Jen hesitated, "Sort of. I can still remember them." Goose pimples came up on her arms as, for a fleeting moment, scenes from the accident flashed through her mind. She immediately experienced a second flash back....the song. The association would be with her for life, and it didn't help that the song was popular. *Brown girl in the ring...*' She shivered slightly and rubbed both her upper arms with up and down motions of her hands. She didn't want to think about her parents anymore. The last thing she needed right now was to start having nightmares about the accident again. In order to forestall any further questions from Rita, she turned to Monique. "What are your parents like?"

"I wish they were both dead," Monique said harshly.

The other two stared first at her, then at each other, uncertain how to react to such an unadorned statement.

"Well, I do," Monique insisted defiantly, then showed a poignant sense of vulnerability when she dashed a hand across her eyes.

"What's the matter," Rita queried, concern mixed with curiosity.

"My mother is leaving us," Monique sniffed. "She met this man, and she is leaving us." She paused, and then added forlornly, "And she doesn't even want me."

"Just 'cause she is leaving doesn't necessary mean she doesn't want you," Jen said, attempting to cheer her up.

Monique however was shaking her head. "Oh, you don't understand my family. My Dad wanted a boy–I already have an older sister, you see, who lives in New York–so the last thing he wanted was another girl. Then I came along, and Mom.... I don't know why she bothered to have children in the first place. She was never a mother to either of us. My sister was lucky. At least Dad noticed her."

"You can't force them to like you," Rita spoke up. "My father didn't want us either."

It was the first time Jen had heard Rita mention her father.

"Did he leave you too?" Monique questioned.

Rita nodded, "He and my Mom weren't married you see. But they had lived together for years. One day–I was about four–he just packed up and left."

"Probably went off with some other woman,"

Monique commented darkly.

Rita shrugged, "I don't know and personally I couldn't care less. If he doesn't want to know me then I certainly don't want to know him. Besides, I really don't remember him well. All I have is a few pictures and a vague memory of someone who used to throw me up in the air."

"I can't imagine not wanting to know my own child," Jen shook her head in wonder. "You mean you have never heard from him since he left."

"Nope."

"Your mother knows where he is." Although stated as a fact, Jen was actually asking a question.

"I'm not sure. I know she knew up to a few years ago and she told us once that she tried to get him to come back shortly after he left, but he simply wasn't interested. He said he needed his freedom and hated being tied down."

"Which just means he didn't want to face up to his responsibilities and wanted to have a good time," Monique inserted.

"Like I said, I don't care what the reasons are. I am not interested in knowing him. He has never supported us; never shown any interest in us; why should I concern myself with him?"

"He is even worse than my Dad," Monique conceded. "At least he stayed and supported us."

"And your mother stayed too so she can't be that bad," Jen pointed out.

"She probably stayed because she got no better offer," was Monique's contemptuous response.

"Monique!" Rita reproved.

"I know what I am talking about," Monique nodded her head, sounding more like a cynical 30-year-old rather than a teenager. "If you met my mother just once you would see. I may see her once or twice a week and it's usually when she is on her way out to some social function or other. I remember when I was smaller and she came in, I would come rushing up to her, you know, to tell her about my day and so on.

She would say," Here she mimicked the high voice of her mother, "'Hello darling, be careful of my dress, go to Debbie now and let her clean you up before you hug me.' By the time I was 'cleaned up' she would be gone.

Sometimes I would ask to be 'cleaned up' just so that I could be clean when Mom comes home. I was that desperate for attention. But it didn't make any difference. She didn't want me hugging her, period! Probably afraid I would crush her dress. Of course, she didn't want to sound uncaring so she would always come up with some petty excuse or other. It was usually my fault. My hands weren't clean enough, or I had a cold and would make her sick, or some speck of dirt on my clothes might rub off on her.... I was about nine or ten when I just gave up. I told Debbie not to even bother calling me when she came in, and if she did ask for me she was told I was busy."

"You mean she accepted that," Rita was skeptical.

"Well," Monique grinned, "Usually when she asked for me that meant she had some of her society friends over and wanted to parade me in front of them. The first time she forced me to come when she called, I created such a scene that she never tried that again. She hates being embarrassed in front of her friends."

"Who's Debbie," Jen inserted as Monique paused again.

"Oh, she is..." Monique paused and actually looked embarrassed before brushing off the question with a wave of her hand. "Debbie is just my maid."

"Oh," Jen cleared her throat and carefully avoided looking at Rita. Rita's mother had worked as a 'maid' for years when Rita was younger. By saving every penny and letting their grandmother look after them, her mother had been able to pay for a secretarial course. What, she wondered, would Monique say to that? She was also curious. There was something else behind Monique's obvious dismissive tone. Monique had sounded embarrassed yet clearly defensive.

"What about other relatives?" Jen asked. She shook her head at Rita's frown, deciding to leave the questions about Debbie for now. "Didn't they care either?"

"Some of them," Monique shrugged, "I have aunts and uncles but it's not the same thing. No matter how much they may love you, knowing that you are living with a mother and father who don't care about you is horrid. You two are so lucky."

Jen wasn't sure she was so lucky. "Have you tried talking with your father," she probed, "Maybe he cares but just doesn't know how to show it."

"I don't see much of him either. He leaves before I get up and is not usually there when I get in. Sometimes when I'm in bed I may hear him drive in. Besides I told you already how he feels about me. He wanted a boy. I have heard that ...oh...hundreds of times."

"Did he definitely tell you that," Rita questioned, "or did Debbie, the maid?" It was clearly a needling question, but it totally went over Monique's head.

"Sure, he did. You two just don't understand," Monique brooded.

There was a moment of silence as they both contemplated Monique's loveless upbringing.

"Have you spoken to your mother since she told you she was leaving?" Jen asked, at last breaking the silence.

"She didn't tell me anything. It was Debbie who told me."

"Oh! Well, did you ask you mother why? I mean, didn't she explain anything."

"No. I didn't ask her anything. Why should I? She didn't even have to guts to tell me herself and had the nerve to ask Debbie to do her dirty work."

There was another silence.

"So, she hasn't spoken to you still," Rita confirmed, beginning to feel uncomfortable with the silence.

"No," Monique was blunt, "So far I have been just ignoring her when I see her."

"Well, Monique, I don't know," Rita shrugged. She was getting a bit annoyed with Monique's self-centeredness. "There really isn't much you can do but accept it if she really means to leave."

"Well once she leaves, that's it. As far as I am concerned, I no longer have a mother. That's the only thing I am going to say to her."

Jen was quite sure that if Monique's mother was as bad as Monique described, nothing would stop her from leaving. After all, the mother would hardly drop her plans just because her seventeen-year-old daughter threatened to disown her. She glanced at Rita to see if Rita had anything else to add.

Rita, on noting her look shrugged again. Monique was dejected and evidently did not want to be cheered up, but rather wanted sympathy. Although sympathetic, Rita and Jen were ready to move on. Discussing the problem further was not helping since they were unable to come up with a solution. Besides, every effort to cheer up Monique was failing.

"I'll ask my mother what she thinks," Rita finally offered. She grinned at Jen as she spoke obviously relishing the thought of Monique taking advice from a former 'maid.'

"Will you?" Monique was grateful, "Maybe she can suggest something."

Jen didn't see how Rita's mother would be able to stop Monique's from leaving. However, if Monique was willing to settle with that, she was not about to upset her further.

"Yes, maybe your mother can help, Rita," she spoke up, cleared her throat, then added, "Let's just finish up this problem, okay."

Rita, also eager to change the subject, quickly accepted, which forced Monique to stop her moping, at least temporarily. They were in the middle of the problem when the bell rang.

Jen cupped her chin in her hands. "Maybe we can finish it up after school," she suggested.

"I have a better idea," Rita said brightly, "We could all go to my home. It's not far from here. We can easily walk and maybe we could play some board games or cards afterwards. You could even speak to my Mom, Monique."

Jen nodded immediately. Monique was a bit more cautious in accepting.

"Debbie usually picks me up," she began hesitantly.

"Why? Can't you drive yourself?" Rita asked with just a hint of sarcasm. Neither she nor Jen had a car and her implication that Monique did was a nuanced dig at Monique's wealth.

"I could. I have my license, and dad bought me a

car for my last birthday, but I hate driving in the city."

Jen gave a choked cough.

Rita nodded sagely. "I would hate driving in the city if I had a car too."

"Yes, traffic is awful!" Monique agreed.

This time Jen could not help laughing out loud.

"What did I say?" Monique demanded looking from Jen to Rita.

"Ignore her," Rita advised. "I don't know why she thinks driving in traffic is fun." Since sarcasm was clearly wasted on Monique, Rita decided on move on. "When Debbie comes you could give her my address and ask her to come back in maybe two, three hours."

They began packing up as Monique thought Rita's plan over.

"Okay," she said, after a while, "That should work."

"See you after school, then," Rita called as she hurried out, "I have a class. I have to go." She stopped abruptly at the door and turned. "Where will we meet?"

"How about at the side entrance?" Monique suggested, "Debbie usually picks me up there. I can tell her then."

The others nodded as Rita left.

Monique looked at Jen. "Are you going to English too?" she asked.

"Yes, but I have to go to our homeroom first to get another book. I forgot it." Jen hoped the excuse would rid her of Monique.

"That's Okay. I'll come with you."

Resigned, yet determined not to retreat into silence again, she joined Monique on the walk to their homeroom. They had just started out when Kim and Marcia approached. Kim waved but Monique completely ignored both her and Marcia.

Jen stared at her.

"It's her brother-in-law's brother that my mother is leaving with," Monique explained, nodding in Marcia's direction.

"Whose, Marcia's?"

Monique nodded, "Kim and Marcia knew that Bob, that's Marcia's brother-in-law's brother, and my mom were seeing. They knew all along and didn't say a word to me."

"Ohh...," was Jen's long-drawn-out response.

She really hadn't noticed that the three had broken up, but then, she had her own problems.

"When did you find out that they knew," she asked curiously.

"Debbie told me. Oh, last night. Then this morning when I mentioned it to Kim and Marcia, Marcia told me that they already knew since Bob was the man my Mom was leaving with."

"Oh. So, you really only just broke up with Kim and Marcia?"

Monique nodded, "I was pretty mad with them when I heard, I can tell you. He has even been around to our house before," Monique continued. "He was always hanging around my Mom, but she has dozens of men hanging around, so I didn't think anything of it."

"What?" Jen was astonished at Monique's casual reference to the mother's affairs. She was not surprised when Monique misinterpreted her shock."

Monique nodded. "That's why I couldn't believe it. Only my mother would bring her lover to her husband's house."

Jen smiled to herself as she expressed her

sympathy. "Since you were all such good friends, they really should have told you, or at the very least mention something." She thought of something, "Maybe they weren't sure…"

"So, Marcia claims, but I wouldn't have kept such a secret from her. And even if she wasn't sure something was going on, she could have hinted, or warned me or something…"

Jen thought a bit and wondered if she should switch sides and suggest that Marcia may well have been telling the truth. After all, if Monique, who supposedly saw her mother with Bob on numerous occasions, hadn't guessed, it was entirely possible that Marcia had not been positive about it. Besides, what friend would want to tell of an affair between her friend's mother and her own relative, especially if there was no positive proof?

"….and she suspected something, or she wouldn't have told Kim."

"Kim said she knew?" Jen was now glad she hadn't opened her mouth.

Monique nodded vigorously, "As soon as I mentioned them, Kim came right out and told me that she knew already."

"Oh... so Marcia was sure enough about the whole thing to tell Kim," she mused. "But isn't Bob younger than your mother. I mean...."

Monique nodded. "Not by much. But I'm sure he is younger. Although Marcia's sister is years older than she is and her sister's husband–his name is John–is the younger brother, I think Bob is younger than my mom. He may not even realize it 'cause my mom looks younger than her age. And I know she would never tell him her actual age."

"Ohh...," Jen didn't know what else to say.

"Right now, I just want her gone."

"Your dad must be feeling pretty bad about it all," Jen was now struggling to keep up her end of the conversation. She wished she could change the subject.

"He would if he had any feelings, besides it serves him right," Monique sounded distinctly hostile. "If he had spent more time at home or caring about us maybe this wouldn't have happened. And for all I know he probably has another woman." After a slight pause she continued, "I hope Bob really messes my mother up. He looks the type too. He's blond like my mom and he's always trying to look and act younger than his age. Huh! They are a pair! More than likely he is just out to have a good time and I know she is just after his money. He doesn't work; I heard his parents left him tons of money. They both deserve each other."

"Hum'um.... well... you mean they aren't getting married?"

"My mother hopes so, but I somehow doubt it. For one thing, the divorce will take a while even if my father doesn't contest it. And he might, just to get back at her. Plus, Bob will soon realize she is just after his money. And who knows, knowing my mother, once she gets accustomed to the alimony, she won't want to lose it. You lose your alimony when you marry again you know," she informed Jen.

Jen didn't know but she nodded in agreement anyway. Thinking about Josie and Uncle Jack she asked, "Can they arrange to have a quick divorce? I mean, maybe they know someone who will arrange to get the divorce sooner?"

"I doubt it," Monique dismissed. "The law doesn't

work that way."

Jen decided not to pursue to point. She didn't want Monique guessing at her reasons for asking such questions. She wanted to change the subject. There was nothing she could do so it didn't make much sense discussing the topic in circles. However, she was too new at conversing with others to effect a subject change with any degree of confidence. She was therefore forced to listen as Monique went on about her parents in general and mothers in particular. Since they were at the Homeroom now, she used the act of getting her books as an excuse to give noncommittal responses.

If she had hoped Monique would leave her once they got to English class, she was soon disappointed. Not only did Monique hang around her for the rest of the day, but she also varied between increasingly vicious comments about her parents and serious bouts of despair. Jen began to hope fervently that Rita's mother would be able to suggest something.

After school, Jen spotted Josie. She turned to Monique, hoping to escape, if even for a little while.

"Will you wait here for me? I forgot to tell Josie to tell our aunt that I'll be late since we're stopping off at Rita's home."

"That's okay, I'll come with you."

Jen had no time to argue, Josie was already disappearing in the crowd of girls streaming towards the exits. She hurried after her. I really should call out to her, she thought as she carefully scanned the crowd. There was the looming possibility that she would lose track of her twin.

Monique obviously had the same impression. As

she hurried to keep up with Jen, she suggested. "Call her. Stop her before she disappears in the crowd."

At first Jen pretended not to hear her. She was afraid she would look stupid if Josie ignored her calls. When Monique again suggested that she call out to Josie she only silently shook her head.

In the end, Monique solved Jen's problems, she shouted Josie's name.

Josie stopped on hearing her name called. She turned around as Monique shouted again and waited impatiently for them to reach her.

"What do you want?" she demanded of them.

"Er... Josie could you tell Aunt Beryl that I'll be home late," Jen began hesitantly. "I'm stopping off at Rita's house," she added.

Josie stared at her. "Who's Rita?" she finally asked.

Jen remembered that Josie knew nothing about her study sessions with Rita.

"You don't know her." Jen felt inordinately proud as she said that. Finally, she had a friend of her own. "She's in commercial six. We study together," she explained.

"Oh!" Josie sounded surprised. "Well, I'll think about it," she decided coolly. She then abruptly turned and walked off before Jen could say anything else.

"What's wrong with her?" Monique asked, remembering that the twins weren't talking to each other.

Slightly embarrassed, Jen muttered, "Oh, I don't know." She wasn't surprised when Monique, put aside her own problems and attempted to question her further.

"Did you two have a fight or something?"

"Something like that," she evaded the issue and now wished that Monique would get back to her own problems. "Maybe we had better go over to the side entrance, Rita should be there already."

Fortunately for her, Monique was too self-absorbed to actively peruse any topic not related to her problems. Jen spent to next few minutes listening as Monique detailed other slights Kim and Marcia had committed against her in the past. It sounded like an endless lifetime of slights to Jen, but she was prepared to accept her defeat by listening politely. The next problem she faced was getting to the exit. They were like salmons trying to go upstream and fighting against the current. With the crowd, walking together or even talking because increasingly difficult. The difficulty solved forced Monique to shut up and fortunately the path did not clear until they were on the major pathway leading to the secondary exit.

Jen spotted Rita waiting for them and in desperation hurried ahead of Monique to forestall a new round of litany. Then, to further avert Monique's tale of woe, as soon as Rita was in talking distance, Jen started a detailed analysis of a prior Math problem. Rita did not even look surprised. She played right along fully aware of the alternative. In any case, fortunately Debbie arrived shortly. The good news was that they were all able to get a ride to Rita's home. Monique of course, arranged to be picked up later.

Chapter 3

Jen was humming softly to herself as she opened the front door. She liked Rita's mom, Ms. Taylor. She was so practical and down to earth. Best of all, you could talk to her, and she would listen, really listen. Even Monique liked her. She had in fact worked wonders with Monique. Monique and Ms. Taylor had a long private chat while Rita and Jen did problems. Monique had seemed much calmer afterwards and definitely less spiteful in her remarks about her parents. Nothing at this stage, however, would cure her self-absorbed nature.

After stepping into the house, Jen half turned to close the door only to stop short. Uncle Jack was sitting on the settee, reading the newspaper. She stared at him in surprise.

"Oh! It's Jen isn't it," he lowered the paper.

Jen nodded, turned and locked the door swiftly then moved towards her room. What is he doing home so early? She thought frantically, then remembered that she was the one who was late. To her shocked surprise, he put down his paper and stood up, starting toward her.

"Josie was in earlier but went to get a few things at the shop."

"Oh," Jen murmured inanely, concentrating on vanishing in her room.

He reached out and casually held her upper arm, effectively stopping her panicky exit.

"Jen...Jen why the rush," he laughed lightly. "When

are you going to grow up and stop acting like a shadow? I don't bite."

Jen felt acutely embarrassed. She took a swift glance at his face then looked down, saying nothing. Why didn't he leave her alone, she thought?

Since usually he virtually ignored her, she felt a shiver of apprehension as he raised his hand and ran it lightly over her hair.

"Don't you think it's time you did something about your hair? Curled it or something? Like Josie's. "

Did he know that she knew? Was that what this was all about? Jen pulled away slightly.

"Please...I...I have to do my homework," she improvised.

"Ahh... So, you do talk. I was beginning to wonder. But I thought you stayed at some friend's house to do just that," he laughed again when she only squirmed, then glanced at his watch. "Run along," he released her and turned back to the living room still chuckling.

Jen breathed a sigh of relief and quickly slipped into her room. She leaned against the closed door and bit worriedly at her lips. What was that all about? As far back as she could remember Uncle Jack had more or less treated her as one would a deaf mute with no means of communicating. He would sometimes go as far as telling Josie to tell her to do something even if she was right there. That he should actually approach her and question her was therefore strange to say the least. She worried her lips for a few more minutes but could come up with no explanation– unless Josie had told him that she knew–that had to be it. Jen wished she had more experience dealing with people. With no clues illuminating Uncle Jack's strange behavior, she finally decided that worrying would get her nowhere and took up her Math's book. They were having elimination matches to choose the quiz team members tomorrow.

A few minutes later she heard Josie get in but made no move to leave her room. She would rather starve than face Uncle Jack again. She was therefore engrossed in her studies when someone knocked on her door.

"Jen!" Josie called. "Jen! Jack says that you're to come out. Dinner is ready."

"I'm not hungry right now," Jen called back, "You two go ahead and eat."

"Jen open the door!" Josie called on turning the knob and finding the door locked.

Jen reluctantly got up and opened the door.

"Jack says that you're to come out," she repeated, flatly.

Jen peered over Josie's shoulder. There was no one in the corridor. "I want to stay here... in my room. Why can't you two eat and leave me? I can always come out later."

Josie stared at her angrily. "What is the matter with you? Jack has noticed that you haven't eating with us for nearly three weeks now."

"Have you told him that I know," she whispered, after taking another quick look behind Josie.

"Yes," Josie admitted defiantly. "I was tired of making excuses for you. If you didn't want him to know then you shouldn't have started avoiding him. I told him about two days ago."

Jen bit her lips. "Josie I can't go out there," she said desperately.

"Yes, you can," Josie said without pity. "You are just embarrassing him with your childish behavior," she added.

Jen shook her head helplessly.

"He said you are just being ridiculous and you're to eat with us from now on," Josie warned.

Jen wrapped her arms protectively about her body. "Can't you talk to him," she pleaded.

"No!" was Josie's unequivocal response. "You may as well come out. He will just come and get you if you don't."

Jen took one last forlorn glance about her room as if seeking help. She finally, reluctantly, nodded.

She followed behind Josie. "I have to wash my hands first," she said as she approached the bathroom.

Josie made an impatient noise. "Well hurry up."

If Jen hoped for a long reprieve, she was to be disappointed. Josie waited as she washed and dried her hands, hurrying her every step of the way.

"I'm ready now," Jen said at last. A condemned would have sounded more cheerful.

Jack was already seated at the table. He smiled at the two girls. "Well Jen it's nice to see your face at diner again," he gestured at Josie, "Start sharing the food, will you?"

Jack kept up a determined string of small talk throughout the meal. He also directed most of his questions at Jen.

She tried monosyllable responses.

That didn't help.

Jack persisted with follow-ups such as 'Yes, what?' or 'Don't look at Josie, I didn't ask her, and I know that you can talk.'

Josie was in fact no help at all. Despite Jen's numerous pleading looks, Josie refused to look at her and, except to pass a comment to Uncle Jack or to answer one of his infrequent questions, barely looked up from her plate.

Jen could not remember ever having had a worse meal. What little appetite she began with soon deserted her. Afraid that if she left her dinner, she would only be inviting more questions, she simply stuffed the food into her mouth as fast as she could. Since she barely chewed the food, she had problems swallowing and used her juice to wash everything down while trying not to choke. She soon started feeling nauseous and silently apologized to her stomach for dumping so much unchewed food in it.

Finally finished, she got up. She vowed to spend the rest of the evening in her room if that is what it took to avoid Uncle Jack. She was about to give her excuse when Josie spoke up.

"It is your turn to wash the dishes," she said, without expression.

Jen had forgotten. "Oh. I guess... I guess I'll come back and do it later." She simply couldn't stay here any longer. Even a short break was better than nothing. As Uncle Jack opened his mouth to say something she rushed on, "Excuse me. I have to go to the bathroom." She pushed her chair in and quickly fled the room.

The next morning, she was in the kitchen preparing breakfast when Josie came in. Jen had not seen her since diner last night. She did not feel it was safe to return to the kitchen until her Aunt got up. By the time even Uncle Jack had given up. Jen had heard him in the study, but he did not disturb her. Josie, she presumed had been in her room. At this point she really did not want to know.

Josie reached up to the cupboards to get the cups and saucers. "You are to eat with us from now on," she stated, without looking at Jen.

Jen nodded. She had already resigned herself to that fact.

Josie did not see her nod. "Did you hear me?" she snapped, swinging around to glare at her twin.

Jen nodded again.

"Well, the least you could do is answer," Josie was obviously fighting for a quarrel.

Jen decided to ignore her. She went to the refrigerator to get the eggs.

Josie, determined to get at response, continued. "Jack is right. You do act dumb. You're so childish."

Jen rounded on her, "You are enjoying this aren't you. You deliberately told him that I knew, knowing that it would make me feel uncomfortable."

"It's your fault. You are the one who started avoiding him. You have no business judging us. We love each other and you're acting as if he has the plague or something," she slammed the cups and saucers on the table. "He practically guessed all by himself. I didn't have to tell him anything."

Jen stared at her then looked away. "I can't help the way I feel. I still think that what you are doing is wrong," she said quietly.

Josie turned her back.

Jen watched her as she set the table. "I still don't see why he wants me at diner with you two," she commented, deciding to change the subject slightly.

She thought that Josie was not going to answer her, but after a few seconds her twin responded.

"Aunt Beryl would soon start wondering why you aren't eating with us," she pointed out, without turning around.

"Aunt Beryl isn't at dinner." Then, "Besides why does he feel he has to question me."

Josie was belligerent again. "You are dumb. Do you know that Jen? You really are dumb."

"What do you mean?" Jen was annoyed.

"I mean that no one likes to be ignored and besides, who are you to judge him anyway?"

"Is that what this is all about?" Jen asked in amazement. "He wants me to like what he is doing? Well...," she broke off as she heard the bedroom door opening.

Josie gave Jen a warning look.

There was silence as they continued the breakfast preparations.

"Good morning girls!" Jack called from the living room moments later. "Anything ready yet?"

"In about five more minutes," Josie called back.

He came into the kitchen, sniffing. "What is it?"

"Fried eggs, fried plantain, and porridge," Josie replied.

"Good." He turned to Jen, "So Jen, how are you this morning?"

"Fine," she muttered.

"Good. Good," Jack repeated, rubbing his hands together as he took his place at the table.

As far as Jen was concerned breakfast was a repeat of the disastrous dinner last night. The biggest difference was that Josie kept trying to engage Uncle Jack in conversation. He ignored her. Jen felt horrible. Whatever was going on she wanted no part of it. Why didn't he answer Josie and leave her alone? Josie soon fell into a sulky silence, which didn't help any. Jen wondered how many more meals like this she would be able to endure.

Jack finished eating first. Although he did not work far, with the morning traffic, Jack had to leave the house by eight as it took him almost one hour to drive to work. The twins meanwhile only had a fifteen-minute walk. He got up smiling then walked over to Josie.

"Bye love," he said, kissing her full on the mouth.

Jen's mouth fell open. She was too shocked to be embarrassed. Meanwhile, Josie, sulkiness forgotten, looked smug as Jack walked out of the room, whistling as he went back into his bathroom.

There was total silence after Uncle Jack left.

Jen, finally finished, got up. "Josie...?" she began.

"If it is anything about Jack and me I don't want to hear it," Josie said without looking up. She raised a hand and tenderly touched her mouth–where Jack had kissed. "Jack loves me."

"But Josie...."

"You know what Jen? You are just jealous because you don't have a boyfriend. No one wants you. Jack says that you have no right judging him and treating him as if he is beneath you. He going to keep needling and embarrassing you and put you in your place." Josie looked up with a satisfied grin to see how her twin would take that.

Jen walked out without saying another word.

Chapter 4

Jen could not so easily dismiss Uncle Jacks actions. How could he kiss Josie in front of me, she thought? Even if they loved one another, did they have no shame? She wondered again if she should tell someone what was going on. But who could she tell? And what could anyone do? Tell Uncle Jack to stop? She did not see that working; besides he was doing it with Josie's consent. Somehow, she felt that the only thing that could stop Uncle Jack would be if her Aunt found out.

Oh, why did this all have to happen? Suppose Uncle Jack really loved Josie and she messed things up for them by telling. Josie would never forgive me, she thought. She sighed, "Maybe I had better leave things for a while and see what happens." She sighed again. Maybe she was just over-reacting. She wished Uncle Jack would leave her alone, though. If only he would ignore her like he used to, she could probable put up with the rest....

Looking up she realized that she had walked on automatic pilot, almost all the way to school. She quickened her steps. Today, after all, was the day of the elimination tests for the Math quiz. Jen shrugged off her problems. She was still excited about the elimination tests and refused to let Josie's affairs distract her. There was nothing she could do. I'll not say anything to anyone yet, she decided. After all, Rita's Mom is the only person she could think of to confide in, and she had only met her once. She would wait. Perhaps after getting to know Rita's mom she would tell her the whole story—not that she felt it would help.

Her decision made; Jen was cheerful as she entered school.

Jen was heading towards her homeroom when Monique called out to her. Jen stopped reluctantly. She didn't think she could cope with Monique's self-absorption today. To her relief however, Monique sounded quite cheerful.

"Hi!" she said, "All ready for the quiz."

"I hope so," Jen smiled.

"It's the first two periods, isn't it?" Monique continued.

"Yes, and they will give us the results by the end of the day."

"Well, good luck."

"Thanks, I'll need it."

She was about to ask Monique if her mother was still leaving when another classmate approached. Jen decided to leave her question for another time. The three girls continued walking and chatting as they made their way to the Homeroom.

Mrs. Miller was already sitting at her desk when they reached. Jen glanced around, looking for Josie. Josie was already in her place. Jen quickly sat down as Mrs. Miller began the attendance roll. After calling the roll, Mrs. Miller looked up.

"Well girls I know I need not remind you that today is the day of the elimination quizzes. You know that you are all eligible to compete, but since only five people will be chosen, you can't all win. However, I wish you all the best of luck.

"Now those participating in the elimination quizzes will meet here right after devotion. That is at eight thirty sharp! And please don't be late. Miss Anderson will be conducting the quiz. The rest of you will of course attend your regularly scheduled classes. Any questions?"

Silence.

"Very well. Please line up for devotion."

After devotion Jen was hurriedly sorting out what she would need for the quiz–pencil, sharpener, ruler, eraser–when Rita approached. Monique had already left for her first class for the day.

She smiled at Rita, "Don't you have any classes this morning?"

"No. Not yet anyway. Are you nervous?"

Jen shook her head, "Not really. It's not like this is an exam."

"I'd still be nervous. Exams... test...quizzes…they are all the same to me. I get a total blackout sometimes. Every scrap of knowledge......it gone." She snapped her fingers, "Just like that."

"You get yourself too worked up, that's why," Jen commented.

"Don't I know! No matter how much I tell myself to relax, my mind just won't listen. I..."

"You had better go," Jen interrupted. "There is Mrs. Anderson coming."

"Okay. I really hope you make it. Bye," Rita hurried out.

Jen gave a sigh of relief as she finished the final problem. She flexed her fingers and looked at her watch.

She still had about ten minutes left. Her eyes quickly roamed the room. Only about two other girls appeared finished and were reviewing their work. She settled down to do the same. She was about halfway through when the final bell rang.

"That's it girls, time is up," Mrs. Anderson called.

Groans and moans were heard throughout the room.

"Could I just finish up this last problem," someone called.

"If you can do it in five seconds, go ahead," was Mrs. Anderson's response. There were smiles as she began timing the seconds. "Okay, come now. Please pass your papers to the front of each row. I will collect them from there. And remain in your seats, please," she added as someone got up.

"Think you made it?" the girl next to Jen asked.

"I don't know. I finished but I'm not sure about two of the problems."

"At least you managed to finish," the girl grimaced, "I needed about fifteen minutes more."

"I needed another full hour," someone else moaned.

Michelle was boasting that she had finished long before the time. Someone tried to shut her up with a sarcastic comment. That didn't work. Michelle didn't even acknowledge the comment. Another girl tried insults. However, Michelle was impervious to insults and sarcasm. It was only one of the biggest problems the other girls had with her.

"Girls! Girls!" Miss Anderson reproved.

With an air of self-righteous vindication, Michelle continued boasting. Behind her, Jen heard someone sniggered. Giving up the counterattack—or probably deciding Michelle could hardly boast if there was no one listening–a group of girls headed for Miss Anderson's desk. There they milled, hoping she would give them preliminary results.

Jen quietly packed up as she listened and watched.

"Seventh period! I said seventh period!" Mrs. Anderson was repeating. "I will not be giving any results before then."

Finally giving up, most of the girls, Jen included, soon left the room.

Jen met Rita and Monique for lunch.

"Please don't ask about the quiz," she begged as they approached.

The other two laughed.

"That's all everyone is talking about," Monique said.

"Don't worry I will find something else to talk about," Rita said with an air of determination. She paused, then, "Have you got any pledges for the walk-a-ton yet."

"I will make about one hundred dollars," Monique said.

"Wow!" Rita exclaimed. "That is more than double what I have so far."

"It's triple mine," Jen admitted. "More than triple probably. How many pages did you fill up?" she asked Monique.

"Not even one really," Monique made a wry face. "I asked my father for thirty dollars outright, and a number of other relative gave me ten and twenty dollars."

"You mean you didn't ask anyone from the school?" Jen asked incredulous.

"No," Monique said, admitting sheepishly. "That would take too long to collect."

"Why didn't you just ask your dad for one hundred dollars?" Rita asked innocently.

"Rita!" Jen reproved. "That's too much money."

"It's not that he wouldn't," Monique shrugged. "I just don't want to compete with Michelle. Kim and Marcia and I discussed it last year. Michelle is just a show-off. She got her mother and Aunt to each give her $100 dollars last year."

"Aren't you lucky you have that option," Rita said. She ignored Monique's grimace.

Jen, reminded of Monique's home problems, asked cautiously, "Has anything changed at home?"

"Nothing," Monique said glumly. "My mother is still leaving. Though I took your mother's advice Rita and spoke to my father," she paused.

"Well! What did he say?" Rita asked.

"He claims he cares about me and don't know how I could have imagined that he didn't," she shrugged. "I have decided to try accepting him as he is. Who knows...? Maybe he really does love me but doesn't know how to show it."

Rita and Jen exchanged uncertain glances. At least this attitude was better than an endless stream of woes, Jen thought.

"Well, at least that's something. Stop worrying about it," Rita consoled. "Like I said, you can't force someone to love you." Then, obviously deciding to change the subject before Monique got dispirited again, she turned to Jen, "So Jen, did you ask your relatives for money too."

"No," Jen admitted. "I only asked the girls here and I haven't even finished one page."

"Not even one page!" Rita tut tutted. "I have

finished three pages."

"So how come you don't have more money?" Monique asked.

"Do you think the girls here are as rich as your relatives?" Rita asked in disbelief. "I think the most I'll get per mile is ten cents. That will work out to three dollars."

"Why don't you get your aunt or uncle to contribute," Monique suggested to Jen. She seemed determined not to fall into gloom.

"Josie asked them already," Jen said quietly.

Rita glanced sideways at her. She had never questioned why Jen and her twin were to longer even on friendly terms.

Monique was not as discrete as Rita. "Surely they would give to you too."

"Probably," Jen was abrupt. Her tone suggested that she had no intention of asking.

Sensing her reluctance to discuss her relatives further, neither girl pressed her. The three of them headed for the canteen to purchase snacks. Afterwards, they found a bench, nicely shared by a Poincietta tree, sat down, and munched on patties, cocoa bread and orange juice.

Jen was quiet throughout most of lunch, content to listen as Rita and Monique discussed the latest movie. She merely shook her head when they tried to draw her into the discussion. She hadn't watched the movie so did not have an opinion. In fact, she couldn't remember the last time she had been to the cinema to watch a movie! Another thing she vowed to change.

The three went their separate ways after lunch. Monique reminded Jen not to leave school without letting her know the results of the quiz.

"Don't leave without telling me whether you made

it or not," Rita also added as she hurried off.

It was not until sometime during the sixth period that Miss. Anderson wrote the names of the five girls who had made the team on the blackboard of the Homeroom. There were also two runners up who would practice with the team and serve as alternates just in case any of the five got sick or couldn't go to any of the competitions.

Surprising, it was Josie who came up to Jen and told her that her name was on the list. They were outside the cottage where English, which was the last class of the day, would be held.

"You made the team you know," Josie said.

"I did?" Jen gave a pleased smile.

Josie nodded and explained about the list Miss. Anderson had placed on the board. Denise, who was with Josie, named the other girls who were on the list. Three of the others were from upper-six forms; including Michelle and two other girls, Mona and Sharon, although Sharon was an alternate. The other three were from lower-six.

"Miss. Anderson wants all team members and alternates to meet her in the upper six homeroom after school," Josie added.

Michelle came over to them. "You heard," she asked excitedly.

Denise nodded, "We just told her."

"I knew I would make it," Michelle boasted. "I was finished long before anyone else."

Josie said in an aside to Jen, "I pity you, with her on the team."

Jen grinned, secretly delighted with the brief communication. This was how they used to be. She almost wished she had never discovered about Josie's and Uncle Jack's relationship.

Michelle, noting their actions if not their words asked, "Oh. Have you two made up?"

Jen glanced quickly at Josie, but Josie scowled and looked away.

Fortunately, Denise decided to break what looked like the beginning of an embarrassing silence. "There are Mona and Sharon!"

They all turned in the direction she was pointing. Monique was also coming from another direction. An excited group formed as the girls continued congratulating each other and discussing the contest to come. They were finally interrupted by the bell marking the beginning of the final period. The forced separation left Jen with a few other girls to enter the building. They were still chatting in groups of twos and threes when the English teacher arrived.

"Okay girls. I know that you are all excited over the quiz team but it's time to settle down. We have only forty-five minutes to complete this lesson."

It was another few minutes before the teacher got complete order and everyone was seated in their places. After that, the lesson proceeded smoothly.

Jen approached Josie after the class. "Will you explain the Aunt Beryl that I will be late," she asked.

Josie nodded. "Sure," she said. "See you later then."

Jen smiled in relief. She knew that their relationship would never be the same again but perhaps something could be salvaged. She turned away and began looking for Monique, finally catching up with her near the commercial six homeroom.

"Oh, there you are Monique," she called. "I'm going over to see if I can find Rita. I know she has probably heard already but she will never forgive me if I leave without telling her."

Monique laughed. "Alright, see you tomorrow."

Jen hurried on. She finally spotted Rita.

Rita, who had also seen her, came up laughing. "I knew you would make it."

Jen grinned, "I have to stay behind to meet with Miss. Anderson."

"Yeah, yeah, I heard," Rita said. "By the way, will we still meet on Monday's and Thursday's during your free period?"

"Of course, with all these matches coming up I will have to study even harder."

"Okay then, see you on Thursday."

The meeting lasted only about twenty minutes. Miss. Anderson congratulated them then went on to say that they would really have to practice hard as a team now. Afterwards she invited questions and they had a short discussion before being dismissed.

When Jen got home her aunt and Josie were in the kitchen preparing dinner.

"Congratulations Jen," Aunt Beryl said, "Josie told me that you made the quiz team."

"Thank you," Jen smiled shyly. She could not help feeling slightly embarrassed in her aunt's presence.

"What did Miss. Anderson say," Josie asked.

"Oh, just routine stuff, congratulating us and making sure we understood about the matches." She turned to her aunt, "I am going to have to stay at school late on Tuesdays and Thursdays. On Tuesdays for the practice and on Thursdays for the matches."

"Don't worry, Josie already explained." Aunt Beryl glanced at the kitchen clock. "Oh dear," she continued, "Can I leave you girls to finish up? I didn't get much sleep today and I am literally falling asleep on my feet." She started out only to stop at the door. "Oh," she added, "I forgot to mention, I have to work overtime tomorrow and on Thursday–the four to twelve shift. So, I'll probably be going out just as you girls are getting in. I'll try to leave everything prepared."

"Sure," Josie said, while Jen nodded.

As her aunt left the room Jen began opening the pots on the fire. Dinner would probably be ready in the next half an hour. Turning to Josie she said, "I will just take a quick shower and start my homework until dinner is ready."

"Suit yourself," Josie shrugged.

Jen left the kitchen.

As Jen prepared for bed that night, she smiled to herself. Things might just work out okay. She would stop letting Uncle Jack's talk get to her. After all, although his talking was uncomfortable, it couldn't hurt her. Surely, she could answer him pleasantly and get through meals with him. This evening he had even seemed to be getting bored trying to drag a normal conversation out of her. She pummeled her pillow and climbed into bed, smiling to herself. Yes. Things would work out. I'll just find some places to go on Saturdays and Sundays.

On Thursday she met Rita and Monique as arranged. They decided not to limit themselves to studying Math alone since Chemistry was Monique's weak subject. Also, with three people, the temptation to gossip was immense so they decided on ground rules. They would spend at least three quarters of the period studying. During that time no talking on things not related to schoolwork allowed.

After school, Jen met with the other team members to practice, and since the real quiz matches would not start until next week Miss. Anderson had them form two teams, three on each side, so that they could conduct mock quizzes. Mona was also elected leader of the quiz team. It was a near unanimous decision, with Michelle being to only girl to disagree with Mona's selection.

Jen was happy as she walked home. Michelle, surprisingly, was quite capable of working as a team member, and apart from being initially disgruntled at not being elected leader, seemed to be fitting in. The credit should likely be given to Mona. She was a no-nonsense girl and although she was petit, no one messed with her. Mona did not mince words and told Michelle bluntly that if she didn't stop boasting she would be voted off the team. Jen was therefore smiling to herself as she inserted the key in the front door. I can't believe this is the same me, she thought as she stepped into the living room.

"Oh hi, Jen," Jack called, as he came into the living room, "I thought you were Josie coming back."

Jen felt a shiver of trepidation. Josie wasn't here? She did not want to handle Uncle Jack on her own.

Seemingly reading her thoughts, Jack continued as he approached her with a smile, "I asked her to run a few errands for me."

Jen had nothing to say. She was not reassured and genuinely anxious as she remembered that Aunt Beryl wasn't here either. She wondered whether she should go back out. That option was taken from her as Jack reached behind her and closed the door.

"What in the world are you so afraid of?" he laughed, "Surely you don't think I am going to attack you."

Jen looked down, shaking her head. She didn't know what to think. She just wished he would leave her alone. She flinched as his hands ran over the top and her head and down her back.

"Come on in! Why are we standing by the door?" He began propelling her towards her room, his hand keeping a light but steady pressure on her back.

"Josie told me congratulations are in order. You made the quiz team."

Jen muttered something. She was hugging her school bag tightly to her chest.

"I'm sure that is not how you respond when questioned at school?" he sounded impatient.

Jen cleared her throat, "Yes," she said, her voice sounding hoarse. "Yes," she repeated in a slightly firmer voice. She tried to stop at her door, but he urged her inside and followed her in. She glanced at the door. He hadn't closed it. Did that mean he was leaving? Could she relax?

"So how did the practice go?"

"Okay," Jen muttered, backing up as he approached again.

He maneuvered her until they were both standing by the bed.

"Sit down for heaven sakes! And stop clutching that bag!" He pried her bag away and dropped it to the floor.

Jen sat, her hands clasped loosely in her lap and tried to relax. Why, oh why, didn't he just leave her alone?

"Jen! Look at me," he turned towards her. When she didn't look up, he used his hand to lift her chin.

Jen kept her eyes down.

"Jen...Jen...?" Both hands were now resting on her shoulders. "Don't you know that I love you?"

Her eyes flew to his in panic. "But...but...what about Josie?"

Jack released her. He took an abrupt turn about the room, running his hands through his hair. "What can I say?" He gave a short laugh. "I guess I used to imagine she was you," Jack admitted.

Jen began shaking her head, "No...no...." She got up.

"Stop panicking." Jack was facing her again, his hands now back on her shoulders. His grip was firm. "I'm not going to hurt you. Look at me Jen. I won't do anything you don't want. I'm not a monster you know."

"Please...please...leave me alone," Jen whispered. He ran the pad of one of his thumbs along her lower lips. She flinched, turning her head away.

"So, my feelings mean nothing to you?"

"I...I just want you to leave me alone," Jen dash a hand across her eyes. She was close to tears. She didn't understand anything anymore.

"Don't cry, my love," he pulled her towards his body.

"No...No!" Jen raised both hands to press against his chest.

He allowed her to maintain a few inches air space between their bodies. "I'm not going to hurt you, you know. Just relax." He was now running his hand up and down her back. "Just relax." He bent and kissed the top of her head. "You are probably hungry. Why not change and then come and have dinner?"

Jen found herself released.

"You still don't believe me, do you?" he asked sadly, noting her fleeting expression of relief.

Jen bit her lips, hoping he would just leave.

"Don't worry. I won't bother you any longer." He turned to go. "I expect you at dinner though. I don't want you starving yourself because of what happened. Okay."

She nodded.

He walked out.

She quickly went over, closed and locked the door. She leaned against it for a moment then rushed over to the bed. She threw herself down and began to cry. What should she do? Should she tell Josie? What could she tell Josie? That Uncle Jack was just using her? She didn't know what to do. It was a while before she stopped crying. She felt a little better although she still didn't know what to do. Jen got up and removed her school uniform. She then took out her books and sat down. For her a routine, even a study routine, was usually very comforting. Yet now she just could not focus, and after a few minutes, of moving from one subject to another she finally put down the books. She just couldn't concentrate on homework, besides she needed to use the bathroom. Was Uncle Jack in his room? She tiptoed to the door and pressed her ear against it. The only thing she heard was the television. That meant he was still in the living room. There was no way he would not see her if she left to go to the bathroom.

Jen felt like stamping her foot. This just was not fair! What do I do now? She needed a distraction to take her mind off her full bladder. Jen grabbed a set of cards from her dresser and went back to her bed. It was a pity she did not have a television in her room.

Jack was still watching the news when Josie came in. Jen listen to them for a few minutes. Josie was talking….

"I got there just as they were leaving."

"Good girl," Jack said.

Jen decided to take a chance. She slipped out of her room and hurried toward the bathroom. She spared a quick glace in the living room only to see Uncle Jack and Josie sitting together on the sofa.

"Do you want to come to my room?" Josie asked.

"No, we'll go to mine," Jack muttered.

Neither of them noticed her…. She liked it that way.

Chapter 5

Jen was back in her room when she next heard her sister. She stood up and went to her locked door. She stood there for a while debating what she should say. Soon she heard Josie leaving the bedroom. Jen opened her door just as Josie went into the bathroom. She took a quick peek into the living room, but Uncle Jack was not there, and within minutes she heard Josie humming as she took a quick shower.

Josie left the bathroom with her towel wrapped about her body and was about to go into the bedroom when Jen called to her.

Josie stared at her twin. Jen was standing in her open doorway.

"What's the matter," she asked impatiently.

"Could you come in for a minute," Jen pleaded softly, "Please...."

Josie came towards her. "Oh. I forgot your practice session was today. How did it go?"

"Fine...fine," Jen said. "That's not what I wanted to tell you." She pulled Josie in the room, closed and locked the door.

"Jen...," Josie began, mystified.

"Just sit down and listen for a minute will you," Jen had decided to tell Josie everything that had happened.

Josie sat at the student's desk while Jen sank down on the bed. "He came in and..."

"Who?" Josie interrupted.

"Uncle Jack!" Jen said flatly, not looking at her twin. She continued, "He came in and started trying to hug me and...and...He was running his hand up my back." She shivered in remembrance and hugged herself. "Then he kissed my...."

"I don't believe you!" Josie jumped up, interrupting.

"I'm telling you the truth." Jen looked anxiously at Josie's angry face, "It's true. He started saying he loves me."

"You're lying." Furiously she came over and slapped Jen's face. "You're lying," she repeated.

Jen stood up holding her face with both hands. She didn't try to hit back. She sniffed. "It's true Josie. I don't know why he did it but..."

"You're so jealous you are now trying to steal Jack away from me," Josie hissed. "Jack loves me! Ever since I told you about him, you've been throwing yourself at him trying to get him to notice you. I don't want to hear any more of your lies," she shouted as she stormed out of Jen's room and rushed towards her own, crying loudly.

"Josie!" Jack called. "Josie! Is something wrong?"

Jen stopped on hearing his voice. She had been about to after Josie. She backup, closed and locked her door softly.

She heard as Uncle Jack came into the passageway. "I thought I heard shouting."

"Jen said...she said...she said… you love her." Josie was crying loud enough for Jen to hear.

"Hush, hush. Jen totally misunderstood what I was trying to say to her. Of course, I love her, but it's nothing compared to what I feel for you. She is such a timid shadow of you. I've been trying to bring her out as it really wasn't good for her, following you around like that. She has to learn to live her own life. I was merely trying to get her to feel good about herself."

Jen could not believe what she was hearing.

"Feeling better now."

Josie must have made some response because Uncle Jack continued. "Just remember, I love you in a special way. I love your Aunt Beryl and Jen too but that's totally different. I'm surprised at you," he said teasingly, "after what we just shared."

"Oh Jack!" Josie buried her face in his chest. "It's just that I love you so. I hate that you have to stay with Aunt Beryl."

"I know, I know. It's only for a little longer, darling. You know I can't do anything about her yet." He paused and Jen imaged him kissing or doing something again.

"Come on," he finally continued. "Put something on and come for dinner. I had better speak to Jen."

"Jen!" He was knocking on Jen's door seconds later.

Jen stood on the other side and watched as the knob turned. Of course, it was locked.

"Jen! Open the door!"

She twisted her hands. What should she do?

"Jen! I said, open the door! I must talk to you." Jack rattled the doorknob slightly.

Jen finally moved. She opened the door.

Jack came in and leaned on the closed door, arms folded across his chest.

"Jen...Jen...," he sighed, then continued softly. "You know your sister loves me. True I don't love her as I love you but since you don't return my love do you think it's fair to destroy what she has?"

Jen said nothing, staring at the floor. As far as she

was concerned, Uncle Jack, in addition to being an adulterer, was a liar and a cheat. She wished that she had the guts to say it to his face. She also wished her sister would stop believing him.

He came over to lift her chin up, but her eyes remained down. "Look at me Jen," he said. He was still practically whispering as he brushed his thumb along her cheek.

She kept her eyes resolutely down.

He laughed softly. "Okay. Have it your way. Just remember that I love you. Your sister merely relieves my frustration right now. I stay with her only because I don't want to hurt her." When Jen did not respond he continued, "I know you don't believe me but if you ask me to, I will stop seeing Josie right now, just to prove it to you."

Jen did not look up.

"Believe me, Jen," he repeated. "I will stop seeing Josie if you ask me to."

He gave a deep sigh and patted her face again when she didn't respond. "I wish I could get you to believe me. Do you want me to promise not to see your sister?"

When Jen still did not respond he finally moved toward the door. "One day you'll believe me, Jen, but for now I'll settle with seeing you at dinner."

Jen stared after him as he left the room. He is trying to use us both, she thought. I should have asked him to stop using Josie and see if he really meant it. She shivered. No. That was much too dangerous; Uncle Jack might expect something from her in return. She sighed. How to get Josie to listen to reason? Maybe she should just leave Josie to her fate. After all, she was already sleeping with him. But if he doesn't really love her then that meant he had no intention of leaving Aunt Beryl and marrying Josie. She sighed again. At least he will leave me alone now he knows I don't love him, and don't want anything to do with him. I'll try once more to get Josie to listen to reason, she decided.

During dinner that night, Uncle Jack virtually ignored Jen leaving her to assume that she was right and that his initial interest had waned. Josie meanwhile basked in his attention and was soon giggling over the silliest nonsense. She too ignored Jen, and Jen was happy to leave them as soon as she possibly could.

The next day Rita bumped into Jen before lunch. She automatically followed Jen to where Monique sat on one of the benches, strategically place below a tree for maximum shade. She noticed that Jen seem preoccupied, and Monique seemed to be dejected again. They all had their regular lunch which was a small orange juice and a patty. The beef patty is a very popular comfort food in Jamaica. It is a golden flaky crust filled with ground beef plus spicy hot Jamaican seasoning. Soon Rita was carrying the entire conversation and although curious, she initially restrained herself and watched as the other two girls used their straws to take occasional sips of their juice. With all that chatting Rita had no time to eat. However, she finally had enough.

"What in the world is wrong with you two?"

"My Dad is shunting me off as usual," Monique said despondently.

"What do you mean?

"He says he has this course he has to attend in America. It's in New York of course, so he'll likely see my sister. I can't stand her…. while I am to stay with his sister and her husband for the next three or four months."

"But Monique," Rita reasoned, "You can't possibly expect him to take you along and if his job is sending him then he probably has to go."

"Oh, you don't understand," Monique said bitterly. "My Dad is vice president of the company. He doesn't have to go anywhere. At least, not now; not at a moment's notice. He just wants to get away from all the gossip since his wife left him, and as usual he didn't even consider me. He just thinks about his first daughter."

"You quarreled with him?" Jen asked curiously.

Monique nodded vigorously. "We had one flaming row last night after he told me. I told him just what I think of him."

"Oh lord!" Rita exclaimed.

"So, what did he say?" Jen asked.

"Oh, he went on a bit about all that he has done for me, but I could tell he felt guilty. Huh! And to think I have been trying to be nice and helpful these past days." She paused then continued defiantly, "Well that's it! I give up. He doesn't really care about me; nothing is going to change that. Well now he can go his way, and I'll go mine. He need not come back for all I care."

"Well, I did tell you that you can't force someone to love you," Rita reminded her.

"I know. I know, but I thought that now, especially since mother is gone, that a least he would notice me more...," her voice trailed off.

"Forget him. If he really doesn't care, your best bet is to forget him," Rita determined. "What about your sister...?"

"I don't know her, and I don't want to," Monique interrupted. "She is supposed to be very smart," she continued disparagingly. "We were never close, and she got a scholarship to an American university right out of high school. It's been three years now and all I get from her is a card at Christmas and one on my birthday."

There was nothing really to add to that, so Rita tried to change the subject and hopefully lighten the mood. "What's your aunt and uncle like?"

"To tell you the truth, I don't really know them," Monique shrugged. "I only meet them at parties and family get-togethers, stuff like that. I have never stayed with them before. I know that Mom didn't like them for some reason. She was always making nasty comments about Uncle Mark whenever his name came up. That's one of the reasons our two families were never close.

"Do they have children of their own?" Jen questioned.

"Yes, two boys aged seven and ten…. I think."

"Look," Rita consoled, "it might work out for the best. You never know. Sometimes things happen that at first seem like the worst thing that could possibly happen and yet it works out in the end."

I can't see any good coming from Josie's affair with Uncle Jack, Jen thought.

Monique wasn't consoled either. "I don't know about that. I just hope they don't treat me like some unwanted garbage. That's all, I hope. Otherwise, I'm leaving. If I have to live with someone other than my parents I may as well stay where I am wanted."

"With who?" Rita asked.

"Our neighbors. They are two sisters, but they are fun. I am going to ask them. Just in case my aunt and uncle don't work out. I'm almost sure that they will say yes."

Rita and Jen exchanged doubting looks.

Monique laughed. "I know them you see. I think I spend more time over there than at my home."

"But will your father agree?" Rita questioned.

"He had better," Monique was grim.

"Well let's hope so," Rita muttered. "By-the-way, what about your mother?"

"What about her?"

"Do you see her? Couldn't you stay with her?"

"Even if she asked me, I'd say no. I haven't seen her since she left. She invited me over one or two times, but I told her I was busy and couldn't come."

"You mean she just accepted that excuse?" Rita was amazed.

"Like I said, you don't know my mother. God knows why she had any children. I got the feeling she was relieved I didn't want to come over."

"There goes the bell," Jen said as the bell rang.

Rita glanced at her watch. "I can't believe the forty-five minutes went already." She turned to Monique, "Well Monique, remember that you promised to give your aunt and uncle a try, which means not going there with an attitude."

"Yeah, yeah."

"I have a class. I have to go. I'll have to finish this later." Rita took two big bites from her patty then picked up her juice. "See you both."

"Bye," Monique called.

"Okay, bye," Jen added. As she hadn't done much talking, she had finished her lunch. She now turned to Monique. "Do you have a class too?"

Monique nodded, hurriedly finishing off her

sandwich. Jen grinned at the comical picture she made with both cheeks stuffed.

"See you later then."

Chapter 6

For the next few weeks, Jen acted more or less like a visitor in her own home. She hadn't been to church often in the past mainly because Josie was usually not interested. Now that getting away from Josie and getting out of the house was her aim, going to church began to appeal. Saturdays she spent at Rita's home. And, after finding out which church the Taylors attended, she was hoping to start spending Sunday's with them at their church.

If Rita or her mother wondered why Jen was practically a permanent weekend visitor, neither commented. In fact, Ms. Taylor made Jen feel very much at home. Jen usually arrived early Saturday morning. Since Saturdays was house-cleaning day at the Taylors, she helped, usually by tidying and dusting the rooms along with Rita. It didn't take that long. The Taylors had a two-bedroom house. Rita and her mother shared one bedroom and Richard, Rita's brother, had the other. There was only one bathroom, placed between the two bedrooms. The other two rooms were the kitchen and a combine living and dining room.

It was on her third Saturday visit that she met Richard. Richard had graduated with an accounting degree from the UWI. Although his regular day job was at a law office in downtown Kingston, he'd been working a temporary job on Saturdays and Sundays in a restaurant. It was vacation coverage for a friend and unless they called him again, he would be free for the next few weeks. He looked nothing like Rita. Jen assumed that he had his father's features and coloring. Rita was short and light complexion like her mother. Richard was tall and much darker. However, he was as friendly as Rita. In fact, she liked him.

They decided to watch television. Jamaica Broadcasting Corporation (JBC) was the only television station, so they did not have variety of options. Ring Ding with Ms. Lou was on. It was a children's show yet MS Lou, Mrs. Louise Bennett-Coverley's, the show's host, was enormously entertaining. Jen especially loved guessing the answer to the riddle and waited eagerly for Ms. Lou's standard question.

"Riddle mi dis, riddle mi dat, guess mi dis riddle and perhaps not."

Richard, like Rita came up with a hilariously funny answer, but he also relentlessly began teasing Jen out of her seriousness. Which was why when the singing started Jen tried to fit in. It was not that she did not like singing. She loved the songs…at least all the songs except one.

Jen cringed when both Richard and Rita began singing along with the Ms. Lou and the children … the one song that she hated. She twice tried to sing too, if only to avoid attracting undue attention, but it seemed not even the threat of embarrassment could get her to frame the words of, "*Brown girl in the ring*' out loud. Richard soon noticed her expression.

"What's wrong?

"Nothing… nothing," Jen tried to shrug it off. "Go on singing," she urged as Rita's voice petered out.

"What's wrong with the song?"

"Nothing….I… I don't know the words…" She

voice trailed off on the lie.

Rita gave her a skeptical look and even Richard looked unconvinced.

"I don't want to talk about it," she finally admitted. "Can we just forget it and enjoy the show."

Fortunately, Richard seemed to understand. He changed the subject by proposing a trip to Hillshire Beach–which was southwest of Kingston–for the following Saturday.

"We can make up a foursome," he added.

"A foursome?" Rita questioned. Richard grinned at her. "Invite Jason, or I will."

Rita made a face at him. Jason was Rita's boyfriend but a few days ago, after going to the cinema, they had a big quarrel and since then they weren't talking to each other. Being Rita, she had aired her grouse before her entire family; an act she always regretted only after the fact. What made the situation worse was that since Jason and Richard were friends, Richard had automatically–in Rita's opinion at least–taken Jason's side.

Jen, who also knew about the quarrel, looked questioningly at Rita.

"Never mind her," Richard interceded on noting Jen's expression. "She and Jason are always quarrelling. This is just the latest in the series. I think they both get a kick out of it."

Rita threw a cushion at him.

He ducked, laughing, "Notice she didn't deny it."

"Only because I refuse to waste my breath responding to frivolous nonsense," Rita said with dignity. She then spoiled the effect by adding excitedly, "Gee! I haven't been to the beach in ages."

"You mean in about two months." Richard corrected. "Didn't Jason just take you?"

Rita flapped a hand at him. "Two months ago! That's ages!" she paused thoughtfully. "Maybe Monique would be interested. Then we wouldn't have to worry about transport. She has a car so she could drive, or her boyfriend could drive. I heard he has a car too, or Debbie could drive us." She grinned. "Oh, to be rich and famous!"

Of the three of them, only Richard has a driver's license and none of them had cars.

"Monique?" Richard asked.

Rita laughed outright. "You will like her…I think. We can't help liking her although she is so taken up with herself. I've never met anyone like her before. Debbie is her, 'maid.'" She made quotes in the air with her hands. "We wondered how Debbie could put up with her but after we chatted with Debbie when she gave us a ride we understood. Debbie acts and sounds like her mother and Monique doesn't have an attitude around Debbie."

"I think Monique gets an attitude because she thinks it's expected of her." Jen commented. She had been sitting quietly throughout their discussion.

"Why get an attitude at all?" Richard queried.

"You have to meet her to understand. Her family life sounds like a soap opera."

Richard did not look as if he was convinced. "Well, I guess it's worth a try asking her," He turned to Jen. "Have you ever been to Hillshire?"

"No," she took her head, smiling shyly. The last time she had been to a beach was five months ago with Josie and some of Josie's friends. Most of the times when Josie planned trips the girls were paired off with their boyfriends and she ended up being the only odd one. It wasn't a comfortable experience and, in the past, she had gone only to please Josie. Josie would be furious with her if she tried to opt out, yet would often ignore her once they got to whatever destination.

"Good. I'll show you all the good spots."

"Good spots for what?" Rita turned laughingly at Jen, "Make sure that it's public spots that he is talking about."

"Ignore her," Richard advised.

Jen grinned. It had been a long time since she had had so much fun. She looked down at her watch. "Oh! I have to go now."

Rita looked at the small clock seated on the bookcase. "Almost 5 o'clock! I didn't realize it was so late," she exclaimed. "Oh blow. Mom will kill me when she gets back. I didn't start dinner." She turned to Richard, "You could have reminded me."

"Me!" he said ungrammatically. "Oh, no. Don't you blame me if you have no memory. Come on Jen, let's get out of here. I'll walk you home.

It was not really dark outside as yet, but Jen did not mind the company. She *really* liked Richard.

Jen was silent on the way home. It was not a strained silence. She simply did not feel the need for small talk. Richard had linked his arms through hers. She looked down. They were almost the same complexion–a rich chocolate brown. She was relaxed even when she became aware of him glancing at her once or twice. Yet he made no effort to engage her in conversation and soon began softly whistling one of the top Reggae songs, in a slightly off-key note. There weren't that many people out, so apart from Richard's whistling only the occasional dog barking or the rumble of traffic on the main roads disturbed the evening.

Jen's steps slowed as they turned onto her street.

Richard glanced down at her again. Although she was tall, he was well over six feet and her head just cleared his shoulder. Jen knew that he was aware that she and her twin had a major falling out but like Rita, he had never pried.

"Is there anyone at home," he asked quietly, on noting her lagging steps.

Jen glanced up at him, startled out of her reverie. She had been trying to think up an excuse for being out so late. "Yes, most likely everyone."

They stopped at her gate.

"What time do you get in from school?" Richard asked suddenly.

"About three, except on Tuesdays and Thursdays. I have the quiz practice sessions on Tuesdays and matches will be on Thursdays. I will get home late then. Maybe about five. Why?"

"Would you like to go to the cinema on Wednesday?"

"Yes!" Jen didn't even have to think about her reply.

Richard grinned at her enthusiasm.

"Okay, I'll come for you here on Wednesday at about six. I don't get off work until five and it may take me an hour to reach here. Is that okay with you?"

Jen nodded, "Yes. That is all right." She started to add something but stopped as a man opened the door of her house from the inside. He did not move from the door. "There's my uncle. I have to go."

Richard looked up. The man was standing at the door frowning at them. "Should I come in and meet him?"

he asked.

"Not now." Jen immediately backed away. "Maybe Wednesday," she said. Maybe never, she thought, no way did she want Uncle Jack to meet Richard. "See you on Wednesday." She turned and ran up her driveway without looking back. She did not see Richard watching with a frown on his face as she rushed in the door.

Although she rushed in, Jen was actually reluctant to face her uncle and stopped as soon as she was inside the door.

"Who was that?" he demanded frowning.

"Rita's brother."

He raised his brows, "I take it he has a name?"

"He is Richard," Jen muttered, she nervously sifted her weight from one foot to the other.

"Richard? Didn't you say you were going to your friend Rita's house?"

"I did. Richard...."

"Is that Jen?" Aunt Beryl interrupted, calling coming from the washroom.

"Yes. Aunt Beryl," Jen answered, glad for the reprieve. She was sure that she didn't want to hear whatever Uncle Jack had been about to say.

"Come in and wash your hands quickly will you Jen. We were about to start eating without you. Why were you so late? Were you at Rita's all this time?" Aunt Beryl had now reached the living room.

"Yes, Aunt Beryl. After we finished studying, we began a game of cards. That is what took so long. I didn't realize it was getting so late."

"And she was walked home by a man who she says

is Rita's brother," Jack inserted. He was frowning as he turned to his wife. "I really don't think she should be spending so much time at these people house. We don't even know them." He turned to Jen, "And I suppose this man was there the whole time."

"No. He works. He isn't there most of the time and he only offered to walk me home because ... well because it was late."

"That's the point I am making Beryl," Jack looked concerned. "She shouldn't be on the streets so late that she has to have an escort home. And God knows who else she may be meeting at this girl's home."

"It's not late… and there was just Rita," Jen protested.

"And her brother. Next time around he may bring home a friend too or Rita may bring home her boyfriend. I think it's best that we put a stop to this before it gets out of hand," he appealed to his wife.

Aunt Beryl was hesitant. It was clear that while she didn't see anything wrong with Jen visiting a friend's house, she didn't want to openly oppose Uncle Jack, especially in front of Jen. "Well Jen, perhaps you could try not staying out so long. You did spend practically the entire day there and this is not the first Saturday you've done it."

"Rita's mother doesn't mind," Jen felt she was being unfairly picked on. And Uncle Jack was a total fraud!

"She may not say anything, but that doesn't mean she wants you underfoot the entire day. And if you go there and there are other people there, especially men, you should leave."

"But Richard lives there, Aunt Beryl." Jen pointed out. "It is more than likely that I will meet him when I go there. I can't simply walk out if I go in and see him there."

"Then maybe you shouldn't go there again. After all, why can't Rita come here?" Jack looked questioningly at his wife. "Seriously Beryl, she has never invited this friend here, yet she spends every spare moment at the girl's house. This is the most lopsided friendship I have ever heard of."

Aunt Beryl still looked undecided. She however concurred. "You are right," she said turning to her niece. "Why not invite Rita here. Afterwards we will see."

"You are all just picking on me." Jen blurted out. "No one has ever said anything when Josie goes to her friends' house or comes home with tons of friends. Josie used to go out with her boyfriend and no one said anything. And no one says anything or asks any questions when she stays at her friend's house until eight or nine o'clock...," she paused for breath.

"There is a big difference here," Jack insisted. "Josie's friends are for the most part merely school age girls or boys. This person I saw you with is no young boy."

Jen began feeling incredible angry. You hypocrite, she thought, staring at Uncle Jack, I am not to go out with Richard, yet you wanted me to see you. You are probably twice Richard's age.

Jack seemed to sense her feelings. He gave her a tight smile but did not back down.

Jen took a deep breath to calm herself. She turned to her aunt. "Could I invite Rita and Richard here then?"

"You can, but it makes no difference," Aunt Beryl is seemed had decided to take her cue from her husband. "At this time, you should be concentrating on your lessons, not in acquiring boyfriends. And you have the quiz matches coming up as well. Besides, I haven't noticed Josie spending all her time outside the house these past few weeks. In fact, I think she has settled down quite nicely..."

Much you know! Jen thought incensed. You haven't even noticed what's happening right under your nose. She no longer felt guilty that Uncle Jack was cheating on her aunt.

"... I think you should do the same Jen," Aunt Beryl continued. "It really would be ridiculous for you to take up where Josie left off and pick up a stream of friends and unhealthy habits. You really should not be spending entire weekends at Rita's house."

"Can Rita come here then?"

"Well...." Aunt Beryl was again hesitant.

"Rita... maybe," Jack inserted, "But I don't think we will be doing her any favors by encouraging her to have a boyfriend at her age." He added, "I know these family scenes. It is just inviting trouble for us to allow you to go on seeing this man." When Aunt Beryl would have interrupted, he insisted, "We really should see how she behaves for a few weeks. If she shows she is seriously studying then maybe we could reconsider."

Jen said nothing. She was afraid that anything she said would lead to further penalties and if she got angry enough, she just might blurt out the wrong things and make matters worse. She had never defied her aunt and uncle before. There had never been a need to. At this point however, she felt that Uncle Jack, of all people, shouldn't be telling her who not to see. Her Aunt Beryl's opinion she simply ignored. Aunt Beryl was just following Uncle Jack's lead.

Aunt Beryl was nodding her agreement. "Ok Jen, show us you are seriously studying and in a few weeks we will see."

Jen simply turned and walked off. This was so wrong. She always studied! She always got good grades! The satisfied smile on Uncle Jack's face was almost more than she could take.

"Let her go," she heard him say to her Aunt Beryl.

It became less easy to hear them as they both made their way into the dining room. Instead of going into her room, Jen opened and closed her room door loudly hoping they would believe that she was inside her room. She waited silently in the passageway to eavesdrop.

"No doubt she is upset that she didn't get her own way." Uncle Jack was saying. "I believe we have to give a little to get a little. She probably feels that by walking off she is defying us and so getting back at us. That's a minor matter. The major problem was this growing affair with that man."

"You are right."

"I have constantly dreaded Josie becoming rebellious and possibly defying me. Never in my wildest dreams could I have imagined having problems with Jen. The amazing thing is that as soon as Josie seems to be settling down and becoming almost house bound Jen has taken up staying out with friends." She paused, "Where is Josie anyway? I haven't seen her all morning."

"In her room studying most likely." Uncle Jack sounded totally indifferent.

"I just can't believe this of Jen of all people. This is something I would have expected of Josie."

"You can never tell with children." Uncle Jack now sounded so moralistic it was downright nauseating. "She is probably a late starter. To tell you the truth I really never noticed her before, she was so silent."

"Yes, I can't understand it. One day she suddenly seemed to come alive and started talking. I still don't know what triggered it."

"I have no idea. You mentioned once that you asked them."

"Yes, but as I told you, Jen said she wanted to lead her own life and Josie told me that she told Jen to stop following her everywhere. Remember it was around the time of the supervisor's exams and I was a bit busy so didn't really pay them any mind," She was obviously trying to justify her acceptance of such a lame explanation. "I just figured they had had a falling out."

Huh? Jen thought. That's just her excuse. She knew her aunt's interest in their lives was minimal at the best.

"Well let's just thank God we picked up on this so quickly, otherwise the next thing we would find out that she's pregnant."

"God forbid!" Aunt Beryl sounded horrified. "You know after their parents died and we had to take them in, that's one of the things I dreaded most—the teenage years. It's one of the reasons I have always preferred boys. At least they wouldn't ever bring home a baby or that sort of problem. Maybe we should just let Jen stay in her room. I really don't feel able to cope with another confrontation tonight."

"Fine with me."

"I'll call Josie then."

Jen slipped quietly into her room. She left her door open a crack and tried listening in to the conversation, but Josie was curiously silent throughout the meal. She didn't comment on Jen absence nor was she informed. Both adults carried out their own desultory conversation making the meal uneventful to the point of boring.

Jen wondered whether there was any point in asking her aunt to allow her to go to Hillshire Beach the following Saturday. The cinema with Richard on Wednesday was definitely out. She decided that tomorrow she would try to catch her aunt alone....

In the end it didn't help. Aunt Beryl was adamant. She refused to give Jen permission to go to the beach. She went so far as to threaten to refuse to allow Jen to go on the walk-a-ton to Hollywell if Jen tried to defy her. In fact, until further notice Jen was no longer allowed to visit Rita's home. Jen was convinced that Uncle Jack was using his influence to punish her.

Chapter 7

Monique was absent from school the next day, so only Rita and Jen met for their regular study session. Jen had only seen Rita briefly that morning. Then Rita had informed her that she wouldn't be able to meet Jen at lunch time since she had to go to the library and finish up a paper that was due today.

"I hope Monique isn't sick," Rita commented as they settled down. Then, "We will have to ask her tomorrow if she can make it to the beach on Saturday."

"I can't go," Jen said flatly.

Rita stared at her, "You can't go? How come?"

"My aunt and uncle decided that I'm picking up where Josie left off and spending too much time away from the house," Jen's didn't care that she sounded bitter. She was still furious. It was *so* unfair.

Rita was still confused, "I don't understand. What do you mean, where Josie left off?"

Jen stared at her books, willing back tears. "Josie used to stay out a lot; she doesn't anymore that's all, and because of that I can't go out anywhere. It doesn't make any sense to me either."

Rita said nothing.

"Could you tell Richard that I can't meet him on Wednesday as we planned," Jen continued.

"Huh? Richard?" Rita was blank.

Jen nodded, she was making nonsensical doodles along her book margin, "He invited me to the cinema on

Wednesday, but now I can't go."

"Oh," Rita smiled, "He didn't tell me. I'll get him this evening." She looked extraordinarily pleased at the news until she saw Jen's expression. "Do you mean you aren't allowed to go anywhere at all?"

"Just to school and back," Jen bit down hard on her lips. She was too upset to even worry about Rita's teasing of Richard. "It's just not fair!

Rita frowned, "I can understand them not wanting you to see Richard. Some parents I know are pretty strict...."

"Well, they aren't my parents," Jen interrupted passionately. She took a deep breath to calm herself, "Look, I don't want to talk about it anymore." Her lips were trembling.

"Ok," Rita agreed quietly, clearly worried. She flicked open her Math book and made a half-hearted effort to find a problem. However, neither of them was in the mood to do problems today. Rita glanced at Jen who wasn't even pretending to find a problem. Jen was just doodling in her book.

"Do you have any relatives in the States, Jen?" Rita asked. She had decided to give up on the studying.

"Huh?" Jen looked up. Rita repeated her question.

"America? I don't think so. Not any close relatives anyway. Why? Do you?"

Rita nodded, "My mother's sister. She is going to file for my Mom and for us."

"Oh! So, you may be leaving soon."

At that Rita laughed, "Not for now. It takes about a year or more for them to process the papers and even then, there are interviews and more stuff to do at the U.S.

embassy here before we can get a visa to leave. My aunt offered to file for my mother years ago, but my mother always refused. She said she didn't want to leave JA., but now Richard's been on at her. He wants to leave. He wants to study law in America. That's why she decided to ask my aunt now."

"So, will you go too?"

"I don't know. I have never been there so I would like to visit... I don't know," she repeated, "Once I get there and see for myself what the place is like, who knows."

Jen nodded, "Do you remember Andrea? She left in forth form."

"Not her alone. There was also...."

They continued sharing their views of America and talking of fellow students who had visited the United States or gone there to live. The bell put an end to their reminiscence. Jen packed up what few books she had taken out as Rita did likewise. At last Jen stood up; she had her arms—with her books—folded across her breast.

"Will you remember to tell Richard?" she asked diffidently.

"Don't worry, I won't forget," Rita promised.

"Thanks," Jen smiled, "I'll probably see you tomorrow. I'll be ok," She added seeing Rita's worried look. "'Bye then."

Rita watched her as she walked out the room.

During dinner that evening, Rita discussed the whole thing with her mother.

"It is so weird Mom. The two of them were inseparable, and Jen never used to say a word. From I was in first form I heard about them. The other girls used to refer to Jen as the silent one–although you couldn't say that and let Josie hear. She didn't want to hear a word against her twin.

I heard that it took so long to get Jen to reply to a question that even the teachers gave up. But because Jen got such good grades no one really did anything. Then one day, about six weeks ago Josie walked in without Jen. This is how I heard it. Talk about shock! Nobody could believe it. Most of the girls thought they had had a fight or something and that they would make up in a couple of hours."

"Neither of them explained what happened?" This from Richard who had been listening intently.

Rita shook her head, "Nope. No explanations given. They barely talk to each other now. Oh! Bye the way, before I forget, Jen says she can't come with us to Hillshire on Saturday, and she can't go the cinema with you on Wednesday. I thought you weren't interested in her."

"Hey, can't I just invite a friend to the cinema." Richard grinned, then asked, "Did she say why?"

"I'm coming to that," Rita made flapping motions with her hands indicating that she wanted him to wait. "Anyway, back to what I was saying." She paused to collect her thoughts.

"They came in separately one day and at first it seemed that Josie was angry at Jen. At least that's how it seemed to me. Jen sort of looked resigned and worried and Josie looked mad. Then a few weeks ago, they seemed to make up. They started exchanging words at school again, and coming in together, although Jen would go her separate way. It wasn't the same as before, but I figured that they had probably made up.

Then, all of a sudden, Josie started becoming the silent one. She now has lunch by herself and doesn't even speak to her friend Denise much now. I know, because after I spoke to Jen today, I checked with a couple of other girls. They told me that the twins have even stopped walking to school together–again. I mean, I can't understand it. And Jen sounded so bitter today, not at Josie mind you, but at her aunt and uncle. I always thought the problem was with her twin, but now it seems to involve her aunt and uncle as well. Oh, and another thing. When we were discussing taking pledges for the walk-a-ton I suggested that she ask her aunt or uncle and she just refused to. She didn't say why she wouldn't either."

"So, what exactly did she say today," Richard asked as Rita paused.

"Oh, just that her aunt and uncle have accused her of taking up were Josie left off and spending too much time away from the house."

"You know, although I didn't want her to feel unwelcome, I did think that it was unusual that Jen was spending practically every weekend here." Ms. Taylor commented. "I suspected something was wrong at her home. However, it may well be that her aunt and uncle just noticed her behavior, tackled her about it and she got upset."

"She was more than a little upset, mom. She was almost in tears." Rita insisted. "I've never asked because I so hate other people prying into my business. Besides you can't force confidences."

"You just said it, dear. You can't force her to tell you anything and whatever it is, unless Jen chooses to confide in you, we will never know. I agree with you that something is wrong, but I don't see how speculating like this is going to help."

"It is just that it is *so* weird Mom."

"It sounds weird to you because you only know a faction of the story. The whole might really be very simply."

"She didn't want me to meet her uncle when I walked her home," Richard said abruptly.

"See, mom," Rita felt justified. "Weird!"

"Did she say why," their mother asked.

"Nope, she just ran off." He shrugged, but Rita could see that he was a bit hurt. After all Jen had spent the entire day at their home.

Even their mother was frowning. "That's not good. Why wouldn't she want her uncle to meet you? That could be why her aunt and uncle have restricted her movement. Any parent would become suspicious if a stranger walked their daughter home and the daughter didn't want them to meet him."

"I think it's more than that, mom," Rita objected.

However, her mother was shaking her head. "Back to my point. Unless Jen talks, it's pointless to speculate."

Rita wanted to continue the argument, but Richard forced a subject change. It was clear that he didn't want to talk about it anymore and as his mother followed his lead Rita was forced to go along. The rest of dinner was spent discussing other topics.

Later as she was brushing her teeth, Richard came up and leaned on the bathroom door.

"Jen has to stay until about five tomorrow, right."

Rita spat the toothpaste in the sink, "Tomorrow? Oh, yes. She has those quiz practice sessions on Tuesdays. I am not sure it they go until five though."

"Her aunt or uncle isn't likely to know that," Richard dismissed, "Will you ask her to look out for me at the main gates at about five?"

Rita frowned. She washed out her mouth before replying, "I'm not sure I should be encouraging Jen to disobey her guardians." She said with a patently fake air or integrity, "After all maybe they just don't want her to have any boyfriends now."

"Come on, Rita," he grinned, "It's too late for you to start getting noble-minded. Besides, you aren't forcing her to meet me. All I want is for you to tell her that I will be there. I just want to talk to her."

"Ok," Rita agreed slowly, then asked curiously, "You are interested in her, aren't you?"

Richard refused to commit himself, "Be realistic Rita, I only met the girl once. I don't know if I am interested or not, I simply want to talk to her."

"If you are hoping to find out why she and her twin quarreled, you can forget it. I doubt that she'll confide in you."

"I'm not going to pry, if that's what you are worried about."

"So, what are you going to talk about?"

"Mind your own business, little sister," his teasing grin took away the sting of the words.

Rita made a face at him, "Don't forget you need me," she warned. "You had better treat me right or your messenger is quitting."

Richard refused to take her seriously. "Ok, I'll leave a particularly big bone for you to chew on," he laughed, reaching over to pat her on the head, something he knew she detested.

Rita pushed him away. "I'll get you for that," she

threatened, as Richard turned away, laughing. "Bye-the-way Richard," she added. "What about the trip to Hillshire? I didn't get to ask Monique since she wasn't at school today."

Richard turned back to face her. "Let's put it on hold for a bit," he decided, after a moment of thought. "Did you tell Jason as yet?"

"You were the one who was going to invite him. I'm not talking to him."

"Sorry, I forgot," Richard looked amused as he walked off.

Chapter 8

Next day when Rita met Jen at lunch she passed on Richard's message.

"Thanks," was all Jen could manage to get out as she bent her head and took a big bite out of her sandwich, while trying to hide her embarrassment.

Rita had no intention of leaving it at that. "I think he's interested in you," she said.

"Who is interested in who?" asked Monique as she approached.

"My brother is interested in Jen," Rita explained.

"Oh, do stop Rita," Jen pleaded. "We only just met once," she continued as she turned to Monique.

"Sometimes it only takes one meeting," Monique then went on to explain how she met her new boyfriend, Mike. "My neighbors invited me to this dinner in New Kingston. Mike was with his parents. He was so cute; I went right up introduced myself."

Rita soon joined in and the two began a lively discussion on the good and bad points of their past and present boyfriends. Jen listened. She had no experience to draw from and was quite content to learn what she could from her friends. Their relationships sounded so normal. Why couldn't Josie find a boyfriend her own age?

"How are things working out at your home" Jen asked during a break in the conversation.

Monique immediately perked up. "I get to live with the neighbors," she smiled. "Dad agreed to let me stay with them!"

"That's great!" Jen turned to Rita and both hugged Monique, sharing her joy.

"So, what happened to you yesterday," Rita asked.

Monique looked guilty. "I overslept and just didn't feel like rushing," she admitted.

"Monique!" Rita made tut-tutting sounds while projecting a disapproving air.

Jen grinned at Rita's actions.

"I don't do it often," Monique excused. "Beside I needed to finish a science project," she confessed.

"Now the truth is coming out," Rita laughed. "You are so lucky you can get away with that. My mom would force me to face up to my crime. That's why I sometime have to spend my free period catching up on homework." She turned to Jen. "I'll bet nothing like that has ever happened to you."

"No," Jen admitted. "I hate last minute rushing, so I generally try to finish all my assignments or projects long before the due date." She also generally finished all homework at home but decided not to add that fact and make her 'crime' worse.

Rita was already rolling her eyes and Monique clutched her chest as if in pain.

"We need to teach you how to procrastinate!"

"I'm at master," Rita offered. "Next time you have something to do, let me know and I'll talk you out of doing it."

Jen ignored their teasing. I can't wait until the end of the day, she thought excitedly.

Richard was standing by the bus stop outside the school gate when Jen emerged.

"Hi!" he called in greeting as he pushed himself away from the wall on which he had been leaning.

Jen grinned shyly at him, then asked hesitantly, "I...I hope you weren't waiting long?"

"Just a few minutes. How was the practice session?"

"Fine. It was fine," Jen didn't know what else to say. She felt bad about not letting him meet her uncle the last time but was reluctant to bring up the subject. He is going to think I'm awfully boring, she thought panicky. She tried to think of something to say but her mind however remained stubbornly blank.

Richard linked his arm through hers and they started walking away from the school.

"I can't go anywhere," Jen reminded him. "I have to go straight home."

"So, I'll walk with you," Richard said calmly. "Partway anyway," he added, seeing she was about to object.

Jen could not relax. "Aren't you going to ask me why I didn't want you to meet my uncle last time?" she finally asked.

"Not if you don't want to tell me." His tone was neutral.

Jen looked up quickly and looked away. "I can't. Not right now. I'm sorry…"

"Sh…sh…. Let's just walk."

For a while they walked in silence. Then Richard began asking her general questions about the quiz team. It took a while, but she was soon relaxed enough to begin conversing normally. She asked him about his work in the law office which stated a candid discussion about jobs and career advancement.

"I want to study law," Richard explained.

"What type of law?"

"Business law. But who knows, I may change my mind once I complete law school. The lawyers I work for mostly handle the legal service for banks and insurance companies and it seems interesting. I do my accounting but I'm always interacting with them. I like it."

"Rita told me you want to go abroad."

Richard nodded, "Yes, the US. The only other option is to Cave Hill campus in Barbados. I'll do that if I have to, but it will be easier to get into a college in the US. What about you? What are you hoping to study?"

"Marine biology. It's not offered at UWI, but I have to get through my natural science subjects there first. I think they offer it at Cave Hill also, but I haven't really checked."

"You have time."

"What's UWI like?

"Fun!" Richard grinned. "Don't get me wrong. We had to study hard to pass the exams, but campus life was fun."

And so their conversation continued. It was so natural to discuss and chat with Richard that, although they took the longer route to Jen's home, it was amazing how quick the journey turned out to be. All too soon, they were turning on Circle Way. Jen's home was almost at the end of the street, but she stopped abruptly. Richard immediately stopped as well.

"Richard…"

"I'll meet you Thursday again, same time, Ok."

"But I'm having a quiz."

"Oh. Where?"

She named the High School. "Usually the school bus takes us to and from the school where the quizzes are being held."

"Like about what time?"

"Usually between five and five thirty."

"Tell you what. I'll wait at your school until five forty-five. If you come after that then you'll know that I already left. Right."

She was hesitant. "But you'll have to wait…and I may not show up."

"I don't mind."

"Richard…"

He stopped her by gently squeezing her hand. "We just met. Let's just get to know each other. Ok."

"Ok…." Jen was still hesitant.

"Stop thinking," Richard grinned down at her. "Until Thursday."

Jen managed to grin back. "Bye then."

"Bye."

They parted.

Jen continued to meet Richard whenever she could, which was mainly on Tuesdays since Thursday meetings did not always work out. To avoid being spotted by anyone who could possibly take stories to her aunt or uncle they soon started meeting not at the school but at a Hero's Park not far from the school. They liked strolling through the park. It was peaceful. Their favorite spot was the newest memorial honoring The Right Excellent Sir William Alexander Clarke Bustamante GBE who served as the first Prime Minister of Jamaica until 1967. They liked that memorial because a huge arch spanned Bustamante's tomb and seats were incorporated at the base of the arch. The seats provide a neat semiprivate area for them to sit and talk. Other memorials honored Jamaicans killed in combat during World War I and II, Marcus Garvey who died in 1940, Donald Sangster the second prime minister who died in 1967 and Norman Manley who died in 1969. Manley, and Bustamante founded the two main political parties in Jamaica, the People's National Party (PNP) and the Jamaica Labor Party, respectively. There were also plans to add other monuments to historical figures.

She no longer went to Rita's house on Saturdays, nor did she invite Rita or Richard home, deciding that it was better to let her aunt and uncle think that she was obeying them. Feelings of rebellion had replaced feelings of guilt, so she no longer felt uncomfortable in their presence. She was also no longer afraid of her uncle, naively assuming that he had decided to leave her alone. She was sure that it was pure spite why he had tried to stop her from seeing Richard. His attitude was that because she wouldn't have anything to do with him, she wouldn't be allowed to see anyone else.

It was Josie who was increasingly causing her to worry. Josie was becoming more and more withdrawn. Jen tried talking to her, but Josie would have none of it. She became aggressive or verbally abusive when questioned. Jen did not give up. She started walking with Josie to school, although they walked in virtual silence. Denise was no longer walking with them. She, along with all of Josie's other friends had given up. I don't like "talking to a dummy" as Denise put it.

She confided in Richard one evening. They were relaxing below the arch of Bustamante's tomb on what had become–to their mind anyway–their bench. It had been just a perfect evening. Richard had been silly and had challenged her to visit each memorial, then meet at the Bustamante memorial in the shortest number of steps. As per rules devised by Richard, they could only follow the paths and could not run.

At the memorial, Richard pulled her in his embrace and gave her a quick kiss on the nose. "I won! I got here first."

Jen's eyes were bright as she stared up at him, "I saw you. You only passed by the Manley memorial. You didn't go up to it."

He kissed her again. "Only because I'm smart. I didn't say we had to actually go up to the memorials just pass by it."

"I was silly to keep going up to every single one, wasn't I," Jen was suddenly serious, as she wondered if Richard thought her stupid.

"Not silly, cute."

Jen push away from him. "I would never have thought of not going directly up to each memorial," she said reflectively. "Even though you did, and I saw you, I just felt I that the rule was to go each one."

Richard leaned back on the seat stretching his legs. "You are a serious person, Jen. There's nothing wrong with that most of the time. I like you for it. But there's also nothing wrong with been silly sometimes."

Jen gave him a wobbly smile. He turned and ran a finger down her nose as he smiled back.

"You know that for years I followed my sister around without talking much."

It was not a question, but Richard answered anyway. "Rita told me, yes."

"I tried to change you know, but it was so hard. Besides, everyone would just ignore me."

"Why did you stop talking in the first place?"

Jen shook her head slowly. "I'm not even sure. I was so afraid. Josie almost died… I felt responsible…."

She did not continue and after a long pause Richard prompted. "Responsible for Josie?"

"No….no…." She abruptly switched focus, hoping Richard would not recognize her deflection. "I sort of feel responsible for her now. She helped me so much in the past but now I just can't understand her. Something must be wrong, but she just doesn't want to talk about it." Jen did not see how ironic it was that she and Josie both used the same approach–both of them kept their problems to themselves.

Richard stared at her for minute then looked away without saying anything.

"I'm probably worrying for nothing," Jen gave a stiff laugh, sadly aware that she had not fooled him. She sensed his withdrawal. The silence was just getting uncomfortable when he asked.

"What does she say when you ask her?"

It was Jen's turn to be silent. She could hardly tell Richard that Josie, when questioned, had accused Jen of trying to break up the relationship between her and Uncle Jack.

"She just won't tell me anything," she finally said, already regretting having started this particular discussion.

Richard looked down at her. He could feel her tension. What was wrong how? He hated this… this lack of trust. He decided to persist for a bit and see what happened. Jen, he noted, had refused to discuss anything of a personal nature before. Up until now he had respected her wishes, but since it was she who had brought up the topic....

"Does it have anything to do with your initial falling out or do you feel this is something new?"

"Yes... I mean no...I," Jen stopped, and began an intent examination of her shoes. When Richard didn't say anything she muttered, "I don't want to talk about it."

Richard ran his hands along the back of his neck in frustration. His relationship with Jen was going absolutely nowhere. She had told him that her guardians wanted her to concentrate on studying for her "A" Levels and that was the reason they didn't want her to have any boyfriends at present. That made some sort of sense. He knew that some parents were very strict and although he felt their attitude stupid, he could at least rationalize it. That was one mistake he hoped he would never make. If he had a daughter, he would rather she brought home all her friends, male or female. That way, at least he knew who she was going out with. So, he had agreed that they would wait until after her exams to go out together, openly. That was ok. He could put up with that for now. It was her secretiveness that he could not take. And this freezing up whenever he asked her a personal question was driving him crazy.

"Look Jen," he said determinedly, "I am not an idiot. I know that there is something wrong between you and your twin, and maybe between you and your aunt and uncle. God knows what it is, and I guess you must feel it's pretty bad since you don't want to talk about it, but that isn't going to solve your problems. You are complaining about your twin keeping secrets, but you are doing the same. Who knows, maybe a second opinion will help. Keeping stuff to yourself certainly hasn't got you anywhere."

"I told you that I don't want to talk about it," Jen retorted. She jumped up.

Richard grabbed her arm and matched her stride as she hurried from the park. "I heard you the first time, but how about considering my feelings for once. We have discussed just about everything except your family. How would you feel if every time you asked me about my family, I told you I would rather not talk about them?"

"You needn't walk home with me if you don't want to," Jen responded awkwardly.

"I see. So, is this how it's going to be?" Richard sounded grim. "What do you plan on doing? Every time a problem comes up in your life are you going to bury your head in the sand and hope that it goes away?"

Jen got mad. "Why don't you leave me alone? You don't know what my problems are, or how I am dealing with them. Just leave me alone. I wouldn't go prying into your business if you didn't want to tell me something. You don't know anything so just leave me alone." She turned to run off, but again Richard stopped her, this time by pulling her into his embrace.

He swore as Jen, her face buried in his shirt, began crying. "Okay, Okay, I'm sorry Jen. I'm sorry." Richard patted her head awkwardly. They were in the middle of the sidewalk, and he felt dreadfully exposed although there were not that many people out. "Come on Jen, let's keep walking," he urged her along.

Richard was silent because he had solved nothing. He knew that he had handled the argument badly. He supposed that a part of his frustration was due to the fact that he hated living with uncertainty. He wanted to get to know Jen better but her refusal to talk to him was leaving him frustrated and angry—angry that she did not trust him. Besides, he could not for the life of him figure out what two sisters could have quarreled over that could be so major.

Once her initial burst of tears was over Jen too was silent. It was not just Richard's questions that had upset her. It was simple that she wished her life could be normal. She wanted her twin back! She could understand Richard's attitude, she had even, more than once, considered telling him the whole story. Yet she was hesitant. She had never been able to bring herself to the point of actually telling him… telling anyone. Perhaps it was because she was ashamed of her twin's behavior and felt that it reflected badly on her. It sounded so sordid, and she was Josie's twin. What if Richard stopped liking her? She really was afraid that Richard would think she is just as bad as Josie. She was such a coward!

By silent consensus, they continue walking straight on to Jen's home. As they reached the corner of her avenue, they both stopped.

Richard sighed heavily and ran his hand across his neck. He took a deep breath and looked up at the sky. Summer was coming so it was still light out. Even so a few stars were now visible. It was going to be a clear night; the moon very close to being full. "It is vast, isn't' it."

Jen followed his gaze, but only nodded.

He took both her hands in his. "We'll work things out Jen."

"I don't know," she sniffed.

Richard gave her a lazy smile. "I do. I like you, so I want to try."

She gave a tentative smile in return as he changed the subject. "It is when I look up at the stars and realize how big this universe must be and what a tiny part of it we take up, that I really feel small. Yet sometimes I feel, so big. Especially on a clear night like tonight, when I feel I can just reach up and touch one of the stars, they seem so close. Even the moon seems close."

Jen gave a hesitant grin, the tension between them diffused. "You're contradicting yourself."

Richard grinned as well, "I am feeling contradictory." Suddenly serious again, he sighed, then admitted, "I really like you Jen." He paused then added, "I'll admit I don't I don't like this situation. But I'm sorry I pressed you like that; it is just that I feel ...well...I guess I just feel that you should trust me more."

Jen looking down as she tried to explain her feeling. "It is not that I don't trust you. It is just that I feel that it is not my story to tell." She bit her lips in indecision then continued, "You see, Josie and I quarreled because she became involved with this man that....is...."

"Totally unsuitable," Richard supplied, as she stopped.

"Something like that," Jen muttered. "She didn't like when I criticized her… the man… anything…"

She stopped and although a million and one questions where were likely screaming to be answered, Richard did not push his luck this time. "Listen Jen, I don't mean to make the same mistake twice. You needn't tell me anything else if you don't want to."

"You won't feel that it is because I don't trust you."

"Actually, I feel much better even though you have only told me that little bit. Don't worry about it. I had better go." He turned to leave, then stopped, "Bye-the-way don't wait for me this Thursday."

"Okay," Jen quickly turned away to hide her hurt, immediately thinking that he had decided to stop seeing her and was looking for an excuse.

"It's not what you're thinking," Richard easily guessed her thoughts. "This has nothing to do with our argument just now. I'm sorry that I didn't mention it before."

"It's all right."

"No, it's not all right. Not if you think I'm trying to back away." He pulled her into his embrace as he continued with his explanation, "There is a cricket match at the stadium on Thursday. Some friends…we all made plans to go awhile back."

"I believe you," Jen reassured him.

"Sure."

She nodded.

"Okay, so I'll probably see you next Tuesday," He gave her hands a quick squeeze. "'Bye then."

Jen was aware of Richard watching her and turned to wave one last time before he took off in the opposite direction.

Chapter 9

That Saturday was the walk-a-ton. Fortunately, the weather was cooperating, and it looked as if it was going to be a lovely sunny day. Jen had progressed with Josie to the point where at least they were again talking to each other. To maintain the truce however they both avoided controversial topics, which meant that Jen still did not know what was troubling Josie. For the time being, she was willing to settle with the status quo.

The girls got up early. They had to meet the rest of the group in Gordon Town by seven o'clock, and Mr. Markland, the teacher who was leading the hike, had warned them that he would not wait beyond seven-fifteen. The hike would take approximately four to five hours and although it would take less time coming back, it did not make any sense leaving later since they wanted to spend at least two hours picnicking once they got to Hollywell. Since it would take over one hour with three bus rides just to get to Gordon Town, Jen and Josie were out of the house by five-thirty. Jack was not up; he had told them not to wake him before leaving and their aunt had not yet arrived home from work.

They arrived in Gordon Town a few minutes after seven, at that early hour the buses were running on half-hour schedules, and they fortunately got off the second bus just in time to see their final connection pulling into the stop. This last connection has a number of girls from their school. Even Josie cheered up and joined the excited chatter. When they disembarked, they found that most of the other girls were already assembled. The group included the two other teachers who were accompanying them.

Jen immediately began looking around for Rita and Monique. She knew Monique would probably get a drive, but Rita had to take the bus and if she was not there now there was no way she would make it in time, as the next bus into Gordon town would not arrive until after seven thirty. They were both there. Jen waved and ran over to join them. She was shocked when Josie decided to join her group even though Denise was there.

However, Jen did not have time to think about how her life and Josie's had reversed roles. Within minutes they were on their way. They were all dressed in jeans with T-shirts and sneakers, and carried their lunch, windbreakers—for the lower temperatures of the mountain, plus assorted odds and ends in back packs, leaving their hands free to aid their climb and maintain balance along the trail. The hike was not really dangerous. However, it did require an experienced guide. There were numerous branching trails and no signage. The trails possibly lead to small cottages or little communities on the mountain, but no one wanted to waste time checking. There were areas where the woods were dense with pine, blue mahoe—the national tree of Jamaica—and other mountain forests. Bamboo and fruit trees abound. Ripe mangoes were scattered around mango trees. One or two of the girls even stopped and picked up undamaged mangos from the ground but unfortunately, they did not have the time to stop and feast. In other areas, the woods thinned, and the trail narrowed past boulder-filled gullies watered by fast flowing streams and mini waterfalls.

There were good-natured groans and teasing as they negotiated the paths and slopes. At one spot they had to cross one of the shallow streams. Some of the girls rolled up their jeans and removed socks and sneaker then waded in. It was a welcome relief –the water being refreshingly cool. Others opted to navigate the stream by stepping on the large boulders that littered the water. There were also a few who just splashed into the water, sock, sneakers and all. Although the water looked clear and clean, they were warned not to drink any. Animals sometimes grazed even here, besides, there was no telling what went on further upstream. After crossing the steam, they stopped for few minutes to put socks and sneakers on. The ones who hadn't bothered with removing their sneakers continued the trek, their sneakers squishing with every step.

At the higher elevations, they noticed lichen, ferns and thunbergia dotting the trees. In some spots they even had an unrestricted view of the steep-sided valleys covered in dense vegetation. It was amazing viewing the doll house looking communities downhill. For a minute Jen stopped and stared as a wave of nostalgia washed over her. It reminded her of cross-country trips with her dad and for the first time the though did not trigger nightmares of the accident. She allowed the others to move ahead of her as she gazed at the view. She wished she had a camera.

As they approached Newcastle, the only pit stop on the journey, the temperature began to drop noticeably. Newcastle, a historic fort, was situated about 3,5000 ft above sea level, and was founded in about 1841 as an alternative training site for British army troops–during the period of Jamaica's colonization. It was now used as a training center of the Jamaica Defense Force. Some of the girls wanted a longer rest but Mr. Markland vetoed that idea. It was only another two hours, three miles, to Hollywell and after a short discussion they decided to take only fifteen minutes break before continuing.

It was close to noon when they reached the Hollywell National Park. Hollywell was at 4,000ft above sea level and in the winter, nighttime temperatures can sometimes fall below freezing. Even though it was the middle of the day, the temperature was still chilly and there was a noticeable mist, obliterating the view below. Since some of the girls had already taken out cameras, they were therefore disappointed, until told that the mist should clear as the temperature rose, which should occur before they left.

There were covered picnic areas with tables and barbecue pits at the park. There were also a few cabins, maintained by the Forestry Department; for these, reservations were required and since they were not planning to stay for the night their group had not reserved one.

More than anyone else, Josie was exhausted by the climb. Jen, Monique and Rita had taken turns helping her along the last stretch of the journey and they and also taken turns carrying her backpack. As she was the only one to require assistance, once they reached Hollywell there was a serious discussion among the teachers on whether she should be allowed to hike back. Josie however insisted that she would be all right after a two-hour rest.

There was a comfortable silence as the two girls made their way up the driveway to their home. Jen began opening the front door, as Josie leaned on one of the columns that supported the covered verandah.

"Still tired?" Jen commented as she watched Josie.

Josie could only nod.

Jen had now opened the door. "Let me help you," she offered reaching for Josie's hands.

Josie brushed her off. "I can make it," she insisted.

Jen went ahead, turning every now and again to watch her twin's progress. She had carried both her bag and her twin, and she now dumped them both on the floor of the living room.

"Are you going to eat?" she asked as Josie turned towards the bedrooms.

"Maybe... later. Right now, I just want to sleep."

"If you eat now, you won't have to get up later."

"Will you stop nagging? I told you I am going to sleep first." Josie was becoming annoyed, and it showed.

Jack, possibly hearing their voices, came into the living room. He was carrying a book, held hanging in one hand, with his first finger between the pages, marking where he had stopped.

"Hi girls. How was the trip?"

"Exhausting," Josie managed a grin.

Jack came over to her and patted her cheek, "You look it." He turned to Jen who had started sliding away towards her room, "So how did you manage, Jen?"

"Fine, really." Then, to divert attention from herself asked, "Is Aunt Beryl here?"

"She's sleeping," Jack responded. "She signed on for some overtime and has to work tonight." He turned to Josie, "Why don't you go take a bath and change while I get something ready for you–for both of you." He added, his look encompassing Jen.

Jen looked at Josie, expecting her to reiterate her

need for sleep but Josie eagerly agreed to Jack's plans. Jen felt she had no choice but to agree as well.

The meal was surprisingly relaxed after all, although Josie was still tired and could hardly keep her eyes open, this, despite Jack's attention.

As soon as Jack left the table Josie immediately stood up, leaving a still half eaten meal.

"Will you tidy up for me Jen?" she asked. "And wash the dishes as well."

"Ok."

"Thanks," Josie yawned, "Gosh, I'm tired. See you tomorrow them."

It was after Aunt Beryl left that Jack made his way to Josie's room. She was sleeping. Without turning on the lights he went and bent over the bed. He kissed the back of her neck to wake her up. She stirred but did not awaken.

"Wake up sleepy head," he called softly, shaking her slightly.

Josie opened one bleary eye, "Oh. Jack." She closed her eyes again, snuggling back into the pillow.

"I know you're tired sweetie, but it's been a frustrating day for me," Jack kissed her again as he climbed into the bed. "Come on Josie, wake up!" He turned her to face him.

Josie groaned in reluctance. Has he always been so inconsiderate? She immediately swashed the thought. He probably had a bad day with Aunt Beryl and just wants me to comfort him. Nevertheless, she was unable to work up any enthusiasm for the act that followed. She was just too tired, and Jack, after an initial attempt to get her to respond simply, 'went about his business.'

Afterwards, fully awake now, she held him close. Should she tell him her suspicions or not? It was now or never.

"Jack..." she began tentatively.

"Hummm."

"I think I'm pregnant."

Chapter 10

"What!!" he jerked away from her. "Are you sure?"

Josie nodded. She was unable to see his expression clearly in the dim light as the room was illuminated only by the moonlight coming in from the windows.

"Where are my things?" Jack got off the bed, looked around, then reached for his briefs which was all he had been wearing.

"I've thought about it," Josie began. "Since I only have a month and a half of school left anyway it won't show, so no one needs to know." She sat up, on the bed and nervously smoothing out her night clothes as she watched him.

Jack was now standing, his back to her as he pulled on his briefs. He said nothing.

"After... after the exams, that is... we could get married."

"I'm still married to your Aunt, remember," he turned around, and was thoughtfully rubbing his cheeks.

At least he is not mad, Josie thought, relieved at his calm tone, "Couldn't we live together until the divorce?"

Jack did not answer her question. "How many months pregnant are you?" he asked instead.

"Two. At least I think so. I missed my last two periods."

Jack swore. "So why didn't you say something before now!"

Josie licked her lips, "I... the first time I kept hoping

it was just late and this month it was supposed to come on Monday... and ... and ..." her voice trailed off.

"Well, you'll have to get rid of it," Jack stated flatly.

"Jack!"

"Listen Josie," Jack sat down on the bed and took both her hands in his. "A divorce... these things take time. It may be two years or more. I'm not really sure. I couldn't openly live with you during that time. The last thing I want is for you to get caught up in the divorce trials, which is what would happen if I lived with you and your aunt found out that you were carrying my child. Now, you wouldn't want that would you?"

Josie shook her head, confused. She had been secretly delighted yet fearful these pass months–from the time she missed her first period. She remembered a girl who had been expelled from school in the fourth form because she was pregnant. She had been terrified that that might happen to her–that everyone would find out that she was pregnant. She had been afraid to tell Jack because this was one of the things that he was careful of. He always used protection, which was why at first she couldn't believe that she was pregnant. But to have Jack's baby! That was so thrilling!

Yet she knew he would be mad when he found out. Still, she had imagined that once she told him, after he got over his initial displeasure, everything would work out. He told her that Aunt Beryl couldn't have children so she imagined that he would be thrilled to have a child of his own. Besides, she had begun to hate this cheating. She felt her pregnancy would at least force things. He would have to divorce her aunt and marry her now; everything would be in the open. Not having the baby… that was something she had never even considered.

Jack was squeezing her hands reassuringly. "Look, everything will be all right. I don't think it is too late. I'll make all the arrangements, and then let you know." Thinking aloud he continued, "It will have to be on a Friday afternoon, that way you will have the weekend to recuperate."

"Oh Jack," Josie's lips were quivering. "I don't want to. I want to keep the baby."

He pulled her head onto his chest as she began to cry. "Shhh...It will be all right. This is the best way you'll see."

"But Jaaack..." she wailed.

"Listen Josie," Jack began firmly, placing a hand on both of her shoulders and putting her slightly away from his chest as her cries reduced to sniffles, "There is no way that you can keep this baby. Why do you think I have always been so careful? In fact, I still don't see how you it could have happened." He paused, "Are you sure it's mine?"

"Jaaaack," Josie began crying again.

"Hush, Josie," Jack pulled her to his chest again. "Hush. I didn't mean that...I am so worried....Anyway, what's done is done. By the way, does Jen know?"

Josie sniffed as she shook her head. "I only told you."

"Good. We had best keep this to ourselves for the moment. In fact, if I can arrange everything this coming week no one need ever know."

Josie looked down. She had her hands clasp tightly together in her laps. "Couldn't the…"

"No!" Jack burst out, interrupting whatever she had been about to say. He had released her and now he stood up. Wiping his hand across his mouth he continued. "There is no way on earth…When we get married, we will have lots of babies. Do you hear me Josie?"

"You don't love me anymore," Jose wept.

Jack sat down again to comfort her. "Josie… Josie how can you even think that?" he said pulling her to his chest. "It's because I love you that I want you to do this. I'm just trying to do what is best for you. Just trust me. We have all our lives to have a baby. Now is just not the time. You need to finish your studies now. I want you to go to college. You don't want to ruin your life now. Babies need lots of attention. You don't have the time to dedicate to caring for one now. But this needn't change anything. Two weeks from now you will wonder what the excitement was all about."

"But I'm so scared."

"I know, I know darling, but everything will be all right." He was running his hands up and down her back.

Josie wrapped her arms about his neck. Apart from the occasional sniff she was quiet now. She had given up—for the moment at any rate—trying to talk Jack into letting her keep the baby.

"You all right now?" he asked.

Josie nodded. She was not all right but she wanted to be left alone. She wanted to think, and she couldn't, not with him here.

"Okay," Jack gave her back a final pat as he got up, "I'll let you know as soon as I have made the arrangements."

Josie just nodded again.

She remained sitting on the bed and must have looked as pathetic as she felt, because before leaving the room he bent over and kissed her again, "Everything will be fine. Just trust me, ok?"

Jack left Josie with a turmoil of confused thoughts. She had been sure that getting pregnant would solve everything. She just felt that it was a perfect pregnancy. She was small and she didn't have any morning sickness. Yesterday on the hike was the first time she felt any different. This pregnancy was just meant to be. She and Jack would get married; everything would be fine. Her mind now skidded away from the unthinkable. Jack loved her! Yet, although he had reassured her of his love, she felt that he should never so callously have wanted to do away with their child and insist on putting off the divorce if he cared for her. If he loved her, he would want her and the baby. But maybe he was scared too.

He loves me. He'll come around; Josie reassured herself.

She felt she had to have this baby, mainly because she saw the baby as her first good chance of getting Jack permanently in her life. She had been so sure… What if he never accepted the baby? What, she wondered, would Jack do if she refused to go along with his plans? Once her aunt found out, what would happen then? Jack would have to marry her then. Even if he didn't right away, he would have to support her. She would be living with him, not here. She knew she would have to leave here. Frankly, she was scared of facing the embarrassment and shame of having the child by herself. What would her friends say? Suppose Jack couldn't come to her right away. Where would she go? She would need money and a job. She didn't know what to do.

She wished she could confide in Jen. But Jen was

being so mean. Most likely Jen was jealous of her. Jen had always been jealous of her. She was the more outgoing twin and people always liked her best.

It was a long time before she felt sleepy, and even so, she spent a restless night. Her dreams were filled with terrifying scenarios. What next?

The next morning Jen was in the kitchen washing up the breakfast things, when Josie came in. Jen was shocked at her twin's wan appearance.

"Josie, are you all right?" she asked.

Josie nodded listlessly, "Where is everybody? "What's for breakfast?" She had just woken up and was not surprised to see that it was close to 11 o'clock. She went over to the stove and opened some of the pots there.

"Uncle Jack took Aunt Beryl to the market and there is okra and saltfish with green bananas." Jen then repeated, "Are you sure that you are all right?"

Josie ignored her twins query. She just did not feel in the mood to talk with anyone. She got a plate and began helping herself to a small serving of the okra and saltfish, she wasn't very hungry even though it was so late.

"You'll probably have to warm up everything," Jen commented as she watched her. "Everything there is yours; everybody else has eaten."

"Okay," Josie emptied the contents of her plate back into the pot and lit the stove. She then took the kettle over to the sink where Jen was standing. Jen moved away and watched silently as Josie filled the kettle with tap water and carried it back to the stove.

"Josie, what's wrong?" she couldn't resist asking again.

"Nothing," Josie said flatly, unwilling to respond. She couldn't tell Jen. Jen wouldn't understand. She ate her meal in silence, aware of Jen's worry and secretly pleased. Jen deserves to be worried. Serves her right! It was her fault. Jack likely wouldn't be so upset with her pregnancy if Jen wasn't acting so righteous. If Jen had falling in love with Jack first, Josie was sure she would have supported her. There was no further talking between the two.

Jen ended up not seeing Richard the next week. He sent a note with a message, via Rita saying that he would be unable to meet her on Tuesday as planned. Jen had a hard time believing he was not still mad at her and explaining away the note to Rita was difficult. By mutual accord, neither Richard nor Jen had told Rita that they were still seeing each other. Not that it mattered now, since Richard seemed to be breaking up with her. Rita, recognizing how upset she was, and for once did not tease. Jen was grateful.

In the end it was just as well that Richard couldn't come. The team met on Tuesday for an unusually long practice session–they didn't finish up until nearly 7 o'clock. The first of the final matches would be on Thursday and if they lost that match, they would automatically place third.

Jen continued walking with Josie to and from school, whenever possible. She was unable to get any information out of Josie, however. She went to Josie's room after dinner on Wednesday evening in another attempt to find out what was wrong.

"Josie the Zoology exam is just two weeks away now."

"So!" Josie was abrupt, she was sitting at her dresser combing out her hair in preparation to put rollers in. She did not turn around.

Jen wondered what to say now. How she wished things were back to normal; that she and Josie were as close as they had been before this all started.

"You said you were going to study," she reminded her twin.

"Just get lost and leave me alone!"

"Josie...."

"Just leave me alone, will you! Leave me alone!" Josie threw the comb on the dresser as she turned and faced her twin. "Get out and leave me alone."

Jen stared at her twin's angry face. "Josie, can't we just forget all the quarrel of the last few months and go back to how we used to be? She was being stilly. She knew it even as the words left her mouth, but she could not help herself.

"You are so dumb!" Josie screamed.

Jen backed out of the room, closing the door as she left.

Josie was right. She was dumb, but she couldn't help wishing things could go back to how they were before. And something was wrong. She guessed that Uncle Jack and Josie must have quarreled since Uncle Jack also seemed preoccupied and began ignoring her again. At least something good was happening!

These days Josie seemed unable to shake off a cloud of depression, and her schoolwork was suffering. The Biology teacher had a quiet chat with Josie after class on Thursday and Jen knew that it was about an unfinished term paper. Only the night before Jen had asked Josie about it and Josie had simple shrugged and said that she couldn't be bothered to set up late just to finish one stupid paper.

Jen began covertly watching Josie when Uncle Jack was around. Could it be that their relationship was falling apart? She hoped so. Josie certainly didn't seem as cheerful around him as she used to.

They lost the match on Thursday. It was a big disappointment for the team, especially after coming so close to winning the championship. A larger than usual crowd of girls had accompanied the team to the match, so it was a dispirited group that slowly made its way back to the school bus. No one felt much like talking. Miss Anderson tried to cheer them up with a pep talk, congratulating them on placing third–it didn't work–so the journey back to Gretagur was completed in relative silence. Even Rita, who had attended every match, was subdued, at least during the bus ride.

As the two made their way home after being dropped off at the school, Rita recovered some of her spirits. Neither Monique, who hadn't been able to come, nor Josie, who had refused to come, were there.

"Well, at least we came in third," she commented.

"Hu'um," was the only response she got from Jen.

"Come on Jen," Rita chided, "Stop moping. We did a lot better than the thirty-three other schools who didn't even place."

"I guess so," Jen sighed... then sighed again.

Rita stared at her in silence for a minute. "Is something else wrong?" she asked.

"No...no...not really."

"Then why the heavy sighs."

Jen hesitated, then said, "It's Josie. I am worried about her."

"Why? What's wrong with her?"

"I don't know. She doesn't look right. And she isn't studying."

"Maybe it's because you two broke up."

Jen frowned at the pavement as she wondered how much she should tell. She finally decided to try half-truths. "No," she said, shaking her head. "It's not that. Something else is wrong. I've tried talking to her, but she won't tell me anything." She looked up, "If she doesn't watch out, she will fail her `A' Levels."

Rita nodded. The `A' Levels started in just two weeks. If Josie wasn't studying now, no amount of last-minute cramming would get her through them.

"She had three subjects. Right."

"Yes, three and General Paper. Physics practical is first. That's in less than two weeks and we also have Zoology and Math."

Rita looked curiously at Jen who was once again walking with her head down. This was the first time Jen had volunteered any information about her twin and their problems. It was too good of an opportunity to miss. She decided to try and see if she could find out why the two had quarreled in the first place.

"So why else would she be upset?" she asked cautiously.

To Rita's surprise, Jen answered. "She is seeing this married man. He says he is going to get a divorce soon, but I don't believe him."

"Blouse and Skirt!" said together like that, it sounded exactly like a swear word. "Do you know the man?"

"Yes." Jen nodded.

"And you say she's still seeing him?"

Jen hesitated, remembering the tense atmosphere at breakfast that morning. "I don't know," she said slowly. "I think they are still seeing each other.... maybe they quarreled though. She has been like this ever since the walk-a-ton and that's over a week now."

"He has probably dumped her," was Rita's opinion. "A lot of these married men, they just want a brief affair. She may have been pushing for them to become more serious and he dropped her."

"Of course, you know all about married men and the affairs they have," Jen teased, smiling slightly.

Rita grinned; she was glad that Jen was now more cheerful. "No. But I have heard enough to know. Who is the guy anyway?"

Jen immediately clammed up. She turned away from Rita, frowning, "I can't tell you."

Rita tried another track. "I don't see why Josie of all people should choose a married man. I mean she was so popular. It's not as if she can't find a boy-friend her own age."

Jen suddenly turned anxious eyes to Rita. A thought had just occurred to her. "You won't say anything to her will you...? or to any of the other girls at school?"

"No, I won't say anything. But someone ought to talk to her. Maybe your aunt. Does she know?"

Jen shook her head.

Rita continued. "It doesn't make any sense; her failing her exams over a man. Why don't you tell your aunt?"

"I just can't," Jen said. She wished Rita was not so persistent.

"Does your aunt know the man," Rita was

undaunted by Jen's obvious aversion to her questions.

"Yes, she does, but she doesn't know that Josie is seeing him."

"You should...."

"Listen Rita," Jen interrupted, clearly desperate to end what was beginning to feel like an inquisition. "There is more to it that. I just can't tell you since it's Josie's story. And I can't tell our aunt; at least not now, not yet."

"Okay," Rita did not sound convinced, "But I still think someone should talk some sense into her."

Jen nodded. She did not hide her relief as she noted that they had reached the intersection, after which they had to go in separate directions. "I'll try talking to her again. Thanks for helping."

"I didn't help," Rita was unusually serious. "I can't even try to help if you don't tell me what's wrong."

Jen nodded again, suddenly feeling teary. She desperately wanted to confine in someone, but she was so afraid of losing her newfound friends. She had been hoping she could tell Rita a part of the problem and perhaps get Rita's help. She now recognized that unless she was prepared to tell Rita the entire story—and she was not—Rita would not be able to help her. Besides, what could Rita do to help? Nothing. "I'm sorry."

Rita hesitated a bit then offered a quick bye in return. Jen hurried off before she could be questioned further.

Chapter11

Classes officially ended that Friday. The school was still open every day for the next month and a half. There were scheduled 'A' level test dates plus the teachers would always be available throughout the normal school hours. Most of the students elected to come to school, using their free time to study. Rita, Jen and Monique agreed to continue meeting at the school. Monique was much happier now that she was living away from both parents. Jen tried inviting Josie to study with them, but Josie declined, saying she preferred to study on her own–a fact that Jen knew to be an outright lie. However, from recent experiences with her twin Jen knew it would be useless to press her.

Jen was afraid of spending too much time at Rita's house on Saturdays. But she so wanted to see Richard. She was therefore pleasantly surprised when he had left a note with Rita.

"Guess who now has a boyfriend," Rita teased as she handed over the note.

"Who, me?" Monique asked. She had been raving recently about her new boyfriend.

"No!" Rita laughed. "Jen! My brother is seeing Jen,"

"Rita, stop," But Jen could not help smiling. She was so please that Richard had contacted her. "We are just friends."

"Yeah, yeah. A boy and a girlfriend."

"How is your new boyfriend?" Jen asked Monique,

hoping that Monique's love of talking about herself would deflect the focus from her.

This time however, Monique did not cooperate. "Oooh! Jen is seeing Richard! Did he kiss you yet?" she asked.

"We've only met in public," Jen tried protesting.

"That's not going to stop my brother," Rita warned. "Just be careful Jen. Don't take him too seriously. He has too many girls."

Jen could feel her cheeks heating.

"He did kiss her…he did!" Monique squealed. "Just look at her face Rita."

There was no stopping them.

"Where did he take you?" Monique wanted to know. "Mike took me to the Marble Grill."

"Get real, Monique," Rita rolled her eyes. "Richard can't afford to take anyone to the Grill."

Jen had heard of the Grill. It was a new upscale restaurant in New Kingston. Seeing another opportunity to stop the questions she asked. "What's Mike like?"

"He is great!" She gave a dreamy grin. "He's black you know. My father is so racist he'll have a fit when he finds out. But Mike is so sweet. He's so dark and I swear his eyes are black. He is 6'5."

"I hope you are not seeing him just to spite your dad," Jen worried, slight shocked at the ease in which Monique had revealed her father's views. But that was Monique.

"Of course not! Debbie asked me the same thing. As far as I'm concerned, I don't have a father."

"What does Mike do?" Jen asked quickly, seeing that Monique was hovering on another bout of despair.

"His father owns a construction company."

Rita rolled her eyes again. "But what does *he* do?" She repeated Jen's question.

"He's in college… I think, or maybe he graduated. I think he helps his father….I'm not sure… I think..."

Jen started laughing.

After that throughout the next two weeks, she met Richard multiple times for lunch since she was unable to stay late after school to meet him. Richard wasn't totally happy with her, but he seemed to have decided not to press her about her family. Jen knew the situation would not last. She was in limbo but reluctant to make any changes so under the pretense of going to school to study, she would head downtown by bus and meet him at his workplace. They would then have lunch together, sometimes in a restaurant nearby, sometimes eating take-out lunch at St. William Grant Park in the center of downtown.

It was a busy park, just south of the North Parade bus terminus and therefore often used as a pathway by people heading to the bus terminus. The park was originally called Victoria Park in honor of Queen Victoria and her stature stood at the eastern entrance to the park. According to folk legend, during the great earthquake of 1907 the statue which had previously faced outwards, turned completely on its base and now faces inwards. In 1977, the park was renamed in honor of Sergeant William Grant. Grant was a well-known labor activist and an associate of Sir Alexander Bustamante, the national hero and former prime minister. The park had other statues. To the south stood the statue of Sir Alexander, while the statue of National Hero Norman Manley is positioned to the north.

This park, in the heart of downtown Kingston, was a lot busier than Heroes Park. There was less privacy so more often than not, they would just wander the streets, chatting. Kings Street, to the south of the park was the busiest street in Kingston with the most store, restaurants, vendors' stalls and banks. If they wanted a more leisurely stroll, they would go to the north end of the park by Ward Theatre which has been in operation since 1777. Every December Ward Theatre opened with the National Pantomime, which was a huge cultural event that usually ran through March or April of the following year. Jen had never seen the show. Richard has once so they both planned to attend this year.

Their next favorite stop was Coke Methodist Church. They would sometime linger there. It was an impression red brick building and stood on the site of the first Methodist church in Jamaica. The church was named after Dr Thomas Coke, founder of the Methodist Missions in the West Indies. The grounds were always open, and they both liked strolling through.

As she left Richard at the top of her street, Jen was figuratively hugging herself with joy. Richard had actually given her a real kiss. She discounted the prior pecks. This kiss had been *real*. They had found a secluded area on the church grounds, and he had sat her down on his lap. He had even touched her breast. She shivered pleasantly just thinking about it. He wanted her. She'd felt him. Now she just hoped the kiss meant as much to him as it did to her. A part of her was afraid because Rita had given her the impression that Richard had lots of girls. Why would he be interested in her? She could dream however, and she was grinning idiotically as she opened the door.

Josie greeted her.

"You weren't at school today, where you?" she asked.

Jen hesitated; she was a very poor liar when asked a direct question. "No," she compromised, "I had to go downtown for something." She started towards her room.

Josie followed her into her room. "Jack went to the school looking for you," she advised.

"Oh," Jen paused, "What did he want?"

"I don't know," Josie lied. She began walking absently about the room and wondered if she should tell her twin that Jack seemed obsessed with her. She was sure he was just trying to teach her a lesson and she was hoping that if she made Jen aware of Jack's interest, Jen would rebuff him, and he would automatically turn back to her.

"What's wrong Josie?" Jen asked.

"I think he wants to use you," she finally said bluntly.

"Use me?" Jen repeated blankly.

Josie nodded.

Jen dropped her school bag to the floor and brushed a strand of hair away from her face. "But...I mean...," she was shaking her head in confusion. "I thought he loved you or you loved him."

"Of course, he loves me!" Josie said abruptly, not for anything would she tell her twin of the violent argument she had had with Jack only yesterday. She had missed her appointment with the doctor. Jack obviously wanted nothing to do with her baby. She however was even more determined to keep the baby. It was her permanent connection to Jack, and she was not about to give it up. Besides, if she had the baby, he would be forced to care of her. He was mad now, but she was still sure he would get over it. She loved him…. He *had* to love her.

She was convinced he was trying to make her jealous by showing an interest in Jen. She didn't know what Jack was going to say when she eventually told him she wanted to keep the baby. She was vaguely hoping he would come up with an alternative solution—like them getting married. She so wanted to get married! Once she was married everything would be alright! He would take care of her and the baby. He would have to. Maybe she could go to another parish where no one knew them. No one would think bad of her then. She knew that she couldn't stay in the house for much longer. She just wished Jack would hurry up–leave aunt Beryl and marry her.

She stopped her wondering thoughts to turn back to her twin. "We quarreled and now he is trying to make me jealous."

Jen was still confused, "So what does he that have to do with me?"

Josie turned away, "You look like me so he thinks he can just use you. I told him that I no longer loved him."

"Well, you can tell him that I don't want anything to do with him."

Jen didn't know what to say. She was quite sure Josie wasn't telling the entire truth. A few months ago, she would have come right out and confronted her. They were no longer that close. She decided to go back to the original topic. "Why do you feel he wants to use me?"

"Because he's been checking up on you. Yesterday he was at the school looking for you and someone there told him that you had left...."

Jen nodded, she had met Rita and Monique at school yesterday morning but later on the three had gone their separate ways and she had gone to see Richard.

"...Well you weren't here when he got in," Josie continued. "Today he came home early and when he heard you weren't here, he left for the school."

"But... but doesn't he have to work.? And why didn't he say something last night? Why is he checking up on me?"

"I don't know. He took time off work I guess, and I told you...."

"Yes ...yes...," Jen interrupted. "But I still don't understand. This doesn't make any sense. I'm not interested in him."

Josie was looking at her nails, faking an involved examination. "I told you. We quarreled and now he feels he has to get back at me. He's just trying to make me jealous and since we are so much alike, he wants to use you and pretend that you are me."

Jen opened her mouth to dispute the fact that they were alike, then closed it again. "Can't you talk to him?" she asked instead.

Josie turned away again.

"I'm mad with him right now. I don't care. I told you. I told him that I don't care and I don't love him."

"Well...er...ah...will you... I mean.... Do you....Have you broken up with him?" Jen finally got out in a rush.

Josie did not turn around. She was obviously flustered which confused Jen even more. This was weird, she thought.

"Oh, grow up, will you Jen," she said with more than a hint of scorn. "This is just a phase he's going through.

Every married couple quarrel and go through this."

Jen wanted to say that they were not married but figured that reminder would not help the situation right now. "Okay," she said slowly. She was still worried–she was now sitting at the edge of her bed. She had so hoped the whole affair was over, then everything could get back to normal. "I wish you would tell him that I am not interested in him. Then maybe he will leave me alone; ignore me like he used to."

"Don't worry about that. Once he realizes that you aren't interested in him, he'll stop teasing you. Just don't encourage him. And don't try to steal him from me."

"You know that I'd never do that!" Jen was appalled at the very thought and wondered if her twin was again going to start accusing her of being jealous. "You know that I am not interested in him, don't you?"

"I am not accusing you of anything," Josie reassured her. "I know he's not really interested in you. He's just mad right now. He could try to use you. But I know he'll come back to me."

"I just want him to leave me alone," Jen was looking anxiously up at her twin.

"I don't see why you are so worried," Josie was suddenly angry. "Maybe he could teach you how to get a man. You should be happy he's showing a little interest in you. He could have any woman and yet he's spending time chasing you. You should be happy."

Jen grimaced at both Josie words and the bitter expression on her face. She had no interest in Uncle Jack and was not interested in any lesson he had to offer either. She decided to change the subject. For her, talking about Uncle Jack was depressing. "I wish these exams were all over."

"So, do I," Josie watched Jen. She began wondering around the room. "It is a pity the subjects are all so spread out."

Jen nodded in agreement. They each had four subjects, General Paper, Math, Physics and Zoology and the Physics and Zoology examinations were divided into two parts. There was the written and the practical exams. They therefore had six days of exams, total but the days were then spread out over a month and a half. So far, they had completely finished only Physics practical and the written Zoology.

"How do you think you're doing so far?" Jen now asked. She was curious, well aware that Josie had not studied much.

Josie shrugged. She had given up on the Zoology and Physics. If she could just sort herself out, maybe she could scrape up a pass on the General Paper and then she might just have a chance with the Math. "I'm hoping to pass Math at least."

"That's in less than three weeks," Jen warned.

"Don't I know it," she turned abruptly to face her twin. "What are you going to do afterwards?"

"You mean after the exams?"

"Yes."

"Go on to the university, I guess? We were both accepted on our "O" Level passes, remember?"

Josie nodded. "You could live on campus," she said thinking aloud.

Jen was puzzled. "Why should I have to live on campus? It's not that hard to take the bus from here to the campus each morning. And aren't you going to the university too?"

Josie didn't answer immediately. How could she say, "I am pregnant, so I won't be able to go, and once our aunt discovers who the baby father is, she will probable kick me out and you as well, just for good measure." After a moment she said, "I don't know if university is for me." Then, before Jen could question her further, she added, "Listen Jen, I had better go and study or I may end up failing even the Math. See you." She quickly left the room.

The confusing conversation with her twin led Jen to forget her initial concern, namely, Uncle Jack's preoccupation with her whereabouts. After Josie left the room, she spent some time speculating on her twin's unusual behavior and hoping that Josie and Uncle Jack were splitting up. But in the absence of concrete proof, she decided her speculations were pointless. Jen went to her desk to retrieve her Zoology notes. She was busy reviewing when she heard first the front door slam, then Uncle Jack's voice.

"Josie... Josie!"

"Yes, Jack," Josie's replied. She must have opened the door just as Jack approached.

"Jen wasn't at the school!" he pronounced grimly. "I talked to some of the girls there and they told me she wasn't there at all today."

"She is in her room. She came in just after you left."

"Oh?" Jack paused. Within seconds Jen's hear a banging on her door. "Jen! Open the door."

Jen reluctantly slid off the bed and opened the door to a furious Uncle Jack.

"You weren't at school, were you? I suspected

something like this when I stopped there yesterday, and you weren't there." He paused for breath. "Where were you?" he demanded. "Answer me," he barked out when Jen remained silent.

Jen sent a pleading look at her twin, standing behind and slightly to the right of Uncle Jack. Josie, however seemed delighted at Uncle Jack's obvious frustration.

Realizing there would be no help from her twin Jen bent her head. "I...I had to go downtown."

Jack stared down at her. He was working hard to control his anger. He wanted to shake her… crush her…or better yet ….. How dare her! He banged his fist against the wall in frustration and swore.

Jen jumped, looking up startled.

"You're lying. If I find that you are sneaking off...," he stopped abruptly and took a deep breath to control himself. It galled him that despite his efforts she was totally immune to him. "I'm going to speak to your aunt about this," he began again, trying to sound authoritative. "You can't be trusted. You are supposed to be using your time constructively studying. We may have to forbid you leaving the house unless you have an exam."

Jen looked rebellious. "I have been studying," she began.

"Oh? And where have you been today?"

"I went window shopping," Jen lied, looking away.

"Stay in your room," Jack ordered. There was no way of proving that she was lying. He slammed the door and turned to find an amused Josie. "So, you think that this is funny, do you?" he queried nastily.

Realizing his mood was dangerous, Josie quickly

smoothed the smile off her face. She shrugged.

Jack's eyes narrowed as he stared at her. He swore to himself, then turned again to Jen's closed door. Finally, abruptly, he swung about, facing Josie again. He gestured to her room. "Let's go inside."

Josie did not move. She was looking up at him, her expression one of aghast.

Jack did not look at her. He was already walking towards her room, concentrating on unbuckling his pants. He was almost abreast her when he noticed her motionless stance.

"Well? Come on!"

"No!" she whispered, shaking her head. "You are just using me!"

"Stop being silly," Jack ordered getting impatient. He griped her arm above the elbow, trying to propel her into the room.

Josie resisted. "I'm going to tell my aunt," she hissed, struggling.

That stopped him for a second. "Don't you threaten me Josie," he warned softly. "You wanted me, remember."

"No...No. I don't want you anymore. You are just using me. You want Jen," her voice was rising.

"Be quiet," he snarled taking a quick glance at Jen's closed door. He opened Josie's room door and dragged her inside, slamming the door behind them.

In Josie's room, Jack had released Josie and was now standing with his arms folded across his chest. "So, what are you going to tell your aunt?" he taunted. "That you're pregnant? That you've been sleeping with her husband? Even if she believes you, she will throw you out."

She had bent her head and was blinking back tears. "You want Jen," she whispered.

"Well, now I want you. And when I want you, I'll call you, and you'll come! You hear me, Josie!" Jack forced her chin up when she didn't respond. "I said, 'did you hear me!'" he challenged.

Josie nodded tearfully.

"I can't hear you," Jack seemed determined to embarrass her.

"Yes," Josie whispered, totally mortified.

But Jack was not finished with her as yet. "Good," he drawled. "Now take off your cloth and get on the bed."

Josie began to cry. "But Jack ...."

Jack was already taking off his pants. "Shut up and get your clothes off," he blazed out.

Crying and sniffing Josie removed her clothes and got on the bed.

Jack totally ignored Josie feelings, bent only on relieving his own frustrations. She did not fight him, but she was upset. She was not ready. He did not care.

Afterwards Josie did not move; she did not make a sound. For a few minutes Jack stayed there, then as Josie turned away crying softly, he got up and got dressed. Josie kept her head turned away from him. Jack watched her as he dressed. He really hadn't meant to use her so harshly. But ....It was so frustrating wanting Jen to like... even now. She was totally ignoring him. Taking Josie was meaningless. He wanted Jen! He had tried wooing her but that didn't work. If he ignored her, she forgot about him completely! Now he was losing Josie too. This was all Jen's fault!

"Look Josie," he said going over to the bed and patting her bare back.

Josie flinched away from him.

Jack tried again, resting his hand lightly on her this time. "Look honey. I guess I was a bit rough..."

Josie remained rigid.

Jack debated what to tell her. He was sure she wouldn't go to her aunt. She had too much to lose, besides, being pregnant she would be too embarrassed. What he really was afraid of was that she might tell Jen!

"Listen Josie, I'm sorry honey. I've been thinking about the baby.... I...I... this is so frustrating for me. Maybe we can figure something out." He jostled her, "Come on, talk to me baby. What do you want me to do?"

As he had expected Josie was immediately encouraged. God she was stupid! She was now looking at him, her eyes wide and teary... yet hopeful.

He gave her a rueful grin. "I'm sorry. It's been so frustrating for me. Forgive me honey....We males can't take much stress and you being pregnant... it's been... I guess I panicked. I know I need to do what's best for you and the baby. Trying to pretend nothing happened was a mistake. I don't know what got into me."

Josie turned to him and began crying in earnest. Jack wrapped his hands around her, "Hush honey. Don't cry. You're killing me here. I'm sorry darling. I never meant to hurt you."

"Oh, Jack," Josie cried.

"Come on. Tell me that you forgive me. What do you want me to do?"

"I want to have the baby and I want us to get married."

Jack took a deep breath. "Ok. I'll cancel the doctor's appointment."

"Jack!" Josie squealed in glee. "Oh, Jack! I love you. I love you so," she squeezed him, pressing her face in his chest.

"Give me a few weeks," he continued, returning her hug. "I'll contact a friend of mine. He's a lawyer. He'll know what's the best way to go about this. I don't want you named as the other woman in my divorce with your aunt. It will prolong things, so we'll keep your pregnancy a secret for now. If everything goes well, I should be able to get a quick divorce. We'll be married before the baby is born. But you must promise not to tell anyone one you're pregnant. Things will get messy if it gets out that I love you. You haven't told your twin, have you?"

"No…no. I didn't tell anyone." Josie's eyes were like stars. She was now gazing at him in delight.

"Good," Jack laughed to himself as he gave her a deep lingering kiss. After giving her a final pat on the back, he smiled and got up and left the room. Ok. He had Josie back. He was frowning however as he came out and saw Jen's closed door. He would have to move quickly. Josie may just have second thoughts, or she might also confide in someone...in Jen.

Chapter12

Josie was finally studying. Jen was delighted. What was not so good was the fact that Josie and Uncle Jack had made up their quarrel and Uncle Jack was now being nice to her–very nice. He told them not to cook and brought home ready cooked meals each evening to allow them more time for study, or so he said. And at dinner, rather than grilling her, he started sharing jokes or telling amusing stories about his childhood. Josie was thrilled and laughed uproariously at his jokes. Jen tried to give a smile and act interested. It was still sometimes uncomfortable, and it wasn't what she wanted but at least he was not being obnoxious about it. Jen figured she could be polite and basically ignore him. The calm lasted a full week.

Josie said she was confident that she had done well on her General Paper and Uncle Jack proposed a family outing to the beach for the upcoming weekend in celebration. The problem was that Rita had been trying to get her to agree to a triple dating trip with her and Monique. She had not yet committed, but definitely preferred a trip with Rita and friends versus going to the beach with Uncle Jack. Besides, she did not want to go on a family outing. She couldn't remember them ever having a family outing. Yet Josie was excited and even Aunt Beryl thought it a great idea.

She came home the next day to find a wrapped

package on her bed. Jen approached her bed cautiously. There was a small note.

From a secret admirer: You're beautiful.

It had to be Uncle Jack. Richard would not send a gift to her home. Lips compressed, she grabbed the package, and without opening it, she threw it in the wastepaper basket. I hope he come in and see it there, she thought viciously. She was violently angry. Why didn't he leave her alone!

That's it! She was not going with them on Saturday. She didn't care what Uncle Jack or her aunt said. They were not *her* family.

Jen got up early on Saturday. She knew the plan was to leave by six in the morning. She helped her aunt and an excited Josie with the beach preparations then deliberately waited until the last minute to announce that she was not going with them. Uncle Jack exploded.

"What do you mean you're not coming?" he literally screamed at her.

Jen refused to budge. "I have a test on Wednesday. I want to stay and study."

"You're deliberately ruining my day!" Josie burst into tears and began screaming. "You're jealous! You're.."

"Josie!" Jack was clearly fearful of Josie's uncontrolled screams. He went over to comfort her, patting her awkwardly on her back as Aunt Beryl looked from Josie to Jen in clear confusion. Jack meanwhile was scowling at Jen. "You are the most selfish…" He turned to his wife. "She knows her sister has been under the weather. That's why I proposed the trip. So, for her to deliberately sabotage it…." He shook his head in disgust.

"You could have mentioned this before Jen," Aunt Beryl still seemed confused.

"I planned on coming but just remembered that I wanted to study some more," Jen refused to feel guilty. Aunt Beryl and Josie didn't really care about her, and Uncle Jack was a hypocrite. No way was she spending a boring day with them.

"So, you wait to tell us now," Jack was glaring at her. "We are ready to go. Why didn't you say something earlier?"

The quarrel dragged on for a few more minutes but Jen was adamant and short of hauling her physically into the car, there was no way for them to force her to go.

"You'll regret this," Jack threatened. He was furious. Jen shivered at the look he was giving her. Fortunately, with Aunt Beryl there his verbal retaliation was limited.

"Leave her." Aunt Beryl was also scowling at her. "Let's go before it gets any later. It really is her loss.

"What's to stop her from leaving the house when we are gone?" Jack asked in frustration.

Jen carefully hid a smile.

"She's seventeen, Jack." Aunt Beryl said impatiently. "So what? She is missing out on a beach trip. Let's go."

Jack gave her another dirty look before admitting defeat. Minutes later the three had driven off.

Jen left the house for Rita's home within minutes of their leaving. She and her friends planned to go to Hope Garden, a botanical garden, which was not too far away. The plan was to get back home before her guardians, so she didn't want to waste a minute of her freedom.

Everyone was there and ready when Jen arrived. She went inside briefly to greet Ms. Taylor before joining her friends. This was Monique's chance to introduce Mike. As she had described, Mike was very tall, with curly black hair, dark eyes and complexion similar to a deep tan. He had a long narrow face, a narrow nose and thin, almost nonexistent lips. What Monique had not mentioned was that Mike was very shy. Jen did not see how outgoing Monique could be attracted to him. She also met Jason for the first time. He was half Chinese, half black.

It was funny. Jen, Rita and Monique got along together fine, even considering Monique's self-centeredness and Jason and Richard were best friends yet the dynamics of all of them together just did not work out.

The first hint of the problems to come began even before they left the Taylor's home. Monique refused to take the bus. The Jolly Joseph, the JOS or Jamaica Omnibus Service was not known for its timeliness, customer service or comfort. Monique wanted no part of it. Rita told a hilarious story how she almost missed her stop. The bus was so crowded she couldn't reach the door to get off. A couple of passengers helped her climb out a window. The story had them all laughing but it just solidified Monique's aversion.

Mike tried halfheartedly to convince her. "Sounds like fun," he said.

"No way am I going on a JOS bus," Monique stated flatly.

He immediately caved. "We will drive."

Mike and Monique had driven over in Mike's car. Monique was fine with that idea.

"What about us?" Rita asked.

"Well, since you like the bus you can take it," Monique, in her typical self-centered fashion saw no problem with her plan. "We can meet you there."

Mike looked embarrassed. "Everyone can ride in my car," he offered.

The problem was Mike's car could only seat four comfortably.

"Look, it's ok. We'll take the bus and meet you there," Richard suggested.

"Why take the bus when we can get a ride. It'll save tons of time," Rita objected.

"Reason number one: we can't all fit in the car," Jason pointed out.

"Some of us could go in my car," Monique suggested doubtfully.

"Is it here?" Jen asked looking around.

"No, it's not," Rita said. "Monique would have to go back home to get it."

"That would take too long." Jen was beginning feel anxious. They were wasting time. "Let's just take the bus."

"I say Monique should get her car," Jason reasoned. "Time wise it will likely work out to be less than us taking the bus."

"No way!" Rita was adamant. "I don't feel like waiting here another hour."

Jason folded his arms across his chest. "So, what do you suggest?"

"I don't know…."

"You don't suggest a change unless you have another option," Jason objected.

"Says who," Rita tuned to glare at him.

"Hold up. Hold up," Richard made cutting motions

with his hands. "Look, it's a half-an-hour drive. We can all fit. The girls can sit on the guy's laps."

Monique gave Mike a teasing look "I like that idea."

"Except you." Richard pointed out. "Mike's driving–no can work."

Monique turned to Mike. "You can let someone else drive, can't you?"

"You can't volunteer a driver for his car," Jason objected.

"I just did. I'm sitting on Mike's lap. Who wants to drive?"

Everyone looked at Mike, but he just shrugged and smiled.

"I'll drive," Richard decided. "Jen will sit up front beside me and you all can take the back seat."

They finally got started.

The gardens were beautiful. Built in the 1880s, and officially called the Royal Botanical Gardens after a visit by Queen Elizabeth II in 1953, its 200 acres of spacious lawns is home to some of the statelier flora and fauna of the Caribbean. The gardens are especially noted for its orchid collection.

Adjacent to the gardens was a small zoo and Coconut Fun Park, an amusement park that opened in the 1960s. It was initially agreed that they would spend the first part of the day in the gardens, go to the zoo then go over to the amusement park to spend the greater part of their day.

That decision did not come easy. In between Monique and Mike necking each other and Jason and Rita arguing, the entire group had squabbled over alternatives options throughout the journey. Finally, Richard suggested a vote.

Yet as soon as they parked, Monique decided she wanted to go to the zoo.

"No," Rita objected. "We decided to go to the gardens first. If we're going to change plans let's do the fun thing first, let go on the rides. That was the second highest vote."

Richard had had enough. "Make up your mind or let's separate. We can meet back at the car at six o'clock or we can all make our own way home."

"Ok. Let's go on the rides," Monique reluctantly agreed. "Although I don't think it fair that Rita gets her way."

Rita ignored her. "Come on, Jason."

Monique and Rita wanted to try everything. Mike went along with just about anything Monique suggested. Jen felt Monique pushed him around too much. It was almost embarrassing, but neither Monique nor Mike seemed to mind. Rita and Jason seemed to have a rule, an hour should not pass without a quarrel.

"Let go on the Bumper cars next?" Rita said after they had completed an exhilarating ride on the scrambler.

"Let's leave the Bumper car until last." Jason disagreed.

"Why?"

"Leave the best for last, I say."

"I agree," Mike said.

"That's a dumb reason," Rita said impatiently. "I say we go on the Bumper car now."

"Yeah, let's," Monique agreed. "Come, Mike."

Mike went without further argument, but Jason continued to protest loudly.

Richard grabbed Jen's hand as she made to follow them. "We'll catch up with you," he called.

Monique turned to wave but Rita and Jason were too busy arguing to notice.

Jen began giggling. "Do they argue like that all the time?"

"Yes, and it gets boring after a while. I must have had amnesia of something. I forgot how bad they are together. I'm now sorry I encouraged them to make-up. Let's get a fudge snack and sit for a while."

That suited Jen just fine. She was with Richard and that was enough for her.

Jen could not remember having so much fun. Although they bumped into the others later, they decided it would be best if they stayed separated. They would meet at Mike's car at six. At four o' clock, exhausted yet contented, Jen and Richard slowly toured the gardens. The gardens, along with other gardens and parks around Kingston, attract a great variety of birds, and Jen was pleased to spot a doctor bird, or streamer tail hummingbird, the national bird of Jamaica. It was a tiny bird less than the length of a hand and found only in Jamaica. The male has two long streaming tails, over six inched in length. Jen loved its beautiful feathers and eagerly watched as the birds dashed from flower to flower, wings beating faster than the eye could follow.

With their tour over, Richard bought them icy mints and they found a bench to sit and relax. Jen ran her hands over the smooth hand railing of the bench wishing that her life was not so complicated. She looked up as she felt Richards's hands in her hair.

"What's wrong?" he asked smiling slightly.

"Wrong?"

"Yes, wrong. You've been rubbing that railing raw; besides you haven't heard a word I said."

"Oh!" Jen snatched her hand away from the railing. She let it fall in her laps.

Richard, applying gently pressure to the back of her neck, pulled her to him and kissed her on her mouth.

"Richard!" Jen jerked back in embarrassment. "Someone will see."

"So, what," he dismissed.

Jen looked around but no one was really paying them any mind.

"See. No one cares," Richard teased, "Can I get another kiss?"

Jen shook her head mutely, putting her hands up to hot cheeks.

Richard grinned at her, then in a spontaneous gesture hugged her, muttering under his breath. "Oh Jen. What am I going to do with you?"

Jen's face was buried in his chest. After a bit, she tentatively reached up and hugged him in return.

"Are you going to talk to me?"

"Richard…"

"Come on," he sounded resigned. "Let's go." He stood and tugged her to her feet. They were both silent as they made their way back to Mike's car.

Jen struggled to keep back tears. Her fun day was ruined.

"It's not my story to tell." She blurted out.

He gave a heavy sigh. "Ok. I accept that. What I can't accept is," he began ticking off on his fingers. "I can't meet your aunt, your uncle or even your sister. I can't come to your house. My sister can't go to your house." He paused,

"Is my mother exempt from the rule?"

Jen bent her head.

"This isn't fair to me Jen. You offer no explanation. How can we have a relationship when you don't trust me?"

"I do trust you," she cried. "It's my family that I don't trust. And they don't want me to see you."

"Why not? You're in sixth form! You're leaving for college soon. It doesn't make any sense."

"I know… I know…."

"Are you saying that you don't know why?"

"I…I…"

"Oh. What's the use?"

Everyone was tired so the journey home was completed in relative silence. Richard focused on driving and Jen spent the time staring broodingly out the window, ignoring the scenic view of Devon House, which a restored nineteenth century mansion, elegantly furnished with genuine antiques and some made-in-Jamaica reproductions. They also passed King's House, the official home of the Governor-General. In Jamaica, the Governor-General is appointed by the Queen of England.

Jen was unhappy but unwilling to break the silence or make the situation worse. Beside the others were in the back. They were too tired to notice that Jen and Richard weren't speaking to each other, but it would be hard to miss a strained conversation.

After his silence in the car, she had thought Richard would simply bid her bye when he got home but he offered to walk her home leaving Rita at the house with Jason. Jason was staying for a while, but Monique and Mike were heading home. Now they walked in silence.

"Do we have time to stop at the park?"

Jen was hesitant. "I think so…"

There were only a few people in the park. Richard led her over to their arch, sat and took both her hands in.

"Jen, I'm sorry."

Jen shook her head. This was it. She felt it. She tried pulling her hands from his, but Richard squeezed her slightly.

"I can't do this anymore…"

"It's ok." With a quick tug she freed herself and ran off. This time Richard did not try to stop her.

Chapter 13

Jen's eyes were swollen when she got home. She had been crying the entire way. Thankfully no one was at home. She went into the bathroom and simple stood under the shower for a while. She couldn't stop crying and as soon as she stepped out fresh tears streamed down her face.

Stop it Jen. Stop it. Crying is not going to bring Richard back. Jen pressed a hand to both eye lids. She took deep breaths and a final shuddering breath. She did not feel any better, but she was all out of tears. She washed her face again and a quick trip to the kitchen got her ice. She wrapped her washrag around the ice. After another face wash, she went to lay flat on her back on her bed and alternated treating each eye with the ice wrap. She was still there when she heard the car pulling up in the driveway. Jen quickly rushed to the bathroom, wrung out the rag and returned to her room. She made sure she was in her room pretending to study when the front door opened.

"Jen! Jen!"

"Yes, Aunt Beryl"

"Come here. We need to talk to you."

Jen reluctantly left her bedroom and met both her Aunt and Uncle in the living room. She took a quick look toward Josie. Her twin was looking smug.

"We've decided on your punishment." Aunt Beryl announced. "I want to see your schedule. For the next two weeks you will only leave the house for your exams."

Jen said nothing. She was not sure how they

planned to enforce the rule, but it didn't matter anyway. Richard had not made any effort to arrange another meeting with her.

"Did you hear your Aunt?" Jack asked.

His aggressive tone indicated he was gearing for a fight, but Jen was too miserable to argue with him.

"Yes," she said without inflection. "Can I go back to my room now?"

Jack would not leave the issue. "I'm going to be checking up on you. You break this rule just one and you'll be sorry. We're the adults here."

When Jen did not respond they were stumped. Jen felt a spurt of satisfaction at the puzzled looks on their faces.

"Can I go back to my room?" she repeated.

"Yes, go," her Aunt waved her away.

"We want your test schedule now," Jack reminded her.

Jen brought the schedule and listened without comment as they outlined her punishment for the next two weeks. She had only the final part of Zoology and Math scheduled for the next two weeks, so basically, she would be stuck in the house all day, every day, except when she was taking those two. She was to return home immediately after each test. Josie was assigned to monitor her comings and goings. The only thing that got Jen mildly upset was the fact that Josie seemed the relish her new role. That hurt. Even so, she did not voice a single objection to their plan. She just did not care.

It was Wednesday of the next week before Jen finally got to go to school for her Zoology practical. It was the first exam that she was not confident about. Uncle Jack had been home both Monday and Tuesday. It was two of the most boring days that Jen had experience in long while. She had mostly remained in her room all of both days because whenever she came out, she had to deal with Uncle Jack. He was trying to be nice to her again and she hated it. The good news was that Josie seemed to have recovered and was more cheerful. Yet it was not their presence that most bothered her. What most interfered with her studies was her repeated mental rehash of her last confrontation with Richard. She kept thinking about what she could have said instead and constantly debated if she should tell him everything. She cringed at the thought. He would likely just think badly of her. Besides, what could he do? Josie was not giving up Uncle Jack anytime soon.

At school on Wednesday, Jen finished her practicum before Josie. She left the classroom quickly, looking for Monique or Rita. After searching all their old haunts, the library, the classroom– she was ready to give up when she spied Monique leaving another exam.

"Monique!" she called.

"Jen!"

The girls rushed toward each other.

"Where have you been? I wanted to tell you about the trip I've planned. When we didn't see you yesterday Rita was seriously thinking about coming to your house."

"I'm grounded!"

"Grounded?" Monique asked as if she didn't know what the word meant.

"You remember Saturday when we when to Coconut Part?" At her nod Jen continued, "I was supposed to go to the beach with my Aunt and Uncle. They are mad that I didn't go."

"That's dumb."

"I know that! Anyway, I'm grounded for this week and next week. I can only come back to school next Tuesday for the Math exam.

"Wow!" Monique looked astonished. "Can parents do that?"

"There is not much I can do to stop them."

"Wow!" she said again. "I would just leave."

"And go where?"

"I don't know. Anywhere."

Jen ignored that. Clearly Monique lived in another universe. "Is Rita here?

"I think so," Monique paused then added. "Mike does have a job."

"What?" Jen was momentarily confused by the change of subject.

"Mike. My boyfriend. He wants to be an engineer. He works in his father's business, doing designs and stuff."

"Oh."

Jen's lack of interest did not deter Monique. She followed Jen into two other classrooms as Jen searched for Rita. Throughout the entire time she continued sharing updates on Mike.

Jen was ready to scream in frustration. She needed to find Rita. As soon as Josie finished, she would have to go. Could she trust Monique to deliver a message?

Defeated she finally went back to sit on a bench close by to her home room.

"….he said we could go. I guilted him into agreeing. So, I'm planning it for four weeks from now. By then we should be finished…"

"What?" Monique's chatter had become background noise and Jen had lost track of the conversation some time ago.

"Weren't you listening?" Monique said, annoyed.

"Can you give Rita a message for me," Jen asked.

"Sure. But did you hear what I said. Dad will pay for the entire trip." She looked at Jen gleefully before adding triumphantly. "For all of us."

"What trip?"

"Seriously Jen, where's your brain today?" It was a rhetorical question and Monique did not wait for an answer. "I got Dad to offer up a graduation gift."

Jen noted that he was now 'dad' not 'father.' She also concluded that it would be less stressful to just focus on Monique for a while. "Did you and your dad make-up."

"Mike said, I should just take what I can get out of him and ignore the rest. Mike…"

"Monique, I have a headache," It was true. She had hoped to find Rita; perhaps send a message to Richard. But tell him what? Jen sighed. "Can you just tell me what your dad did or is going to do?"

"He is paying for us to go the Cayman Islands. Four nights. All-expense paid. It's that great!"

Jen looked at her in amazement. "He agreed to that?"

Monique nodded eagerly. "Yes, for all six of us."

"Wow!" Then she remembered that Richard was no longer talking with her. She turned away, troubled "I don't know if Richard will come…He's not seeing me any longer."

"Of course, he is. He gave me and Rita a message to give you. We were wondering where you were yesterday and Monday. I told you. Rita was thinking of going to your house."

It was pointless getting mad with Monique. That would just invite hypertension. Jen however, could not keep the irritability from her tone. "What's the message?"

"I have it in my bag. I can't get it now. We'll have to wait until the exam is over. So, we will have to plan a date."

"A date?"

"When to go. Jen, what's wrong with you? You aren't paying attention."

It flashed in Jen's mind that Monique's father may have ignored her for a reason. Upset with herself for the uncharitable thought, she mentally counted to ten before responding.

"My head," she said faintly, clutching at her temples. In truth her headache was seriously getting worse.

"Oh! I don't have anything for headaches. We will have to get everyone together to figure out a date."

Jen bent over, holding her head in her hands. "Please, Monique. Can you wait until we meet up with Rita to discuss this?" She was trying to figure out how to get the note from Monique and perhaps respond without being seen by Josie. Spy stuff... if only she could find the enthusiasm for it. The only thing cheering her up was the thought of telling Richard what she had to do just to get a message to him. He would have a fit laughing, she thought wistfully.

"Sure. But since you are grounded that will be almost two weeks from now. Can't you sneak out or something?"

"I'll try." She looked up in time to see Josie leaving the classroom. Josie looked strained. Jen stood up. "The class may be empty now. Let's go and check."

Monique move to follow just as Josie approached. "You have to come with me," she told Jen abruptly.

"Monique has to get something for me. I'll catch up with you." She did not give Josie a change to respond. She grabbed Monique's hand and hurried her into the classroom.

The message was from Richard.
I want to see you,
Richard

Jen quickly scribbled her situation on the back of the note then handed it back to Monique. "Can you make sure he gets it? Please Monique. It's important. I really have to go. I will be back next Tuesday for sure."

"I'll give it to Rita when I see her," Monique promised.

Jen nodded, gave Monique a quick hug and hurried off. She felt much better. She also trusted Monique to deliver the note, eventually. She could grin now as she thought about the last few minutes with Monique. She felt much happier. Richard wanted to see her again. Did she dare hope that he loved her? She knew that she loved him but introducing him to her family was out of the question. However, she vowed to tell him more. Hopefully he would understand.

Uncle Jack was home when she got in.

"So how did the exam go girls?" he asked.

"Oh, Jack…" Josie gave a tearful look, raising her arms as she approached him.

Jack backed away; clearly afraid she was going to

throw herself at him. "Your Aunt is here," he warned.

Josie dropped her arms. "I messed up," she said hopelessly. "I just couldn't concentrate."

Jen started sliding toward her room.

Jack turned from Josie without responding. "Jen! I spoke to your Aunt. I decided to lift your punishment, so you are no longer grounded. See how nice I am?"

If he expected Jen to show him gratitude, he was doomed to be disappointed.

"Thanks," she said politely and turned to walk to her room.

"Is that it," Jack queried angrily. "I begged your Aunt to reduce your punishment and all you can say is a measly, thanks?"

Jen could have said, 'I didn't ask you to,' but she was too happy to start an argument with Uncle Jack. She shifted from one leg to the other and glanced at Josie who was looking sulky because of the lack of attention.

"Well?" he demanded.

"Jack…!" Josie wailed.

Jack gave her an impatient look before turning back to Jen. Jen however was almost at her room. "Where do you think you're going?"

"I need to study," Jen said.

He was clearly frustrated but unsure what to do.

"Jack… Jack…"Josie interrupted again. "I don't feel well."

"Josie!" Jack glared at her.

Josie immediately burst into tears. She ran sobbing to her room. Jen gave Uncle Jack a scorching look before following Josie. However, Josie began screaming at her as soon as she entered the room.

"Leave me. Leave me. I hate you!"

Jen turned to leave only to find Jack at the door. He caught her by the arm before she could slip by.

"This is your fault," he hissed trying to pull her closer.

Jen doubled her fists and struck him on his chest with both hand as she repeated her sister's words. "Leave me alone. Leave me."

"Jack?" Josie had turned to look at them.

Jen got a brief glance at Josie tearful face before Uncle Jack released her. She ran to her room slamming the door behind her. She quickly turned the lock then stood with fists clenched by her side. Why didn't he leave her alone, she agonized?

Chapter 14

Surprisingly, no one called her out for dinner that night. She sneaked out of her room much later to use the bathroom. There was silence from Josie's room and all the lights were out, so she assumed that everyone was asleep. Jen went back to bed vowing that nothing would stop her from going to school the next day.

Early the next morning she listened as Josie got out of bed and started breakfast. Jen was reluctant to leave her room but felt guilty not helping Josie. She finally decided, got up and after a quick wash, went to the kitchen.

"'Morning, Josie" she said. Josie was getting something from the cub-board and did not turn around.

"What are you fixing?" Jen ask as Josie took a pot to the stove.

No answer. In fact, Josie refused to look at Jen. Jen stared at her for a minute then shrugged. It was highly frustrating, but they managed to work around each other with the breakfast preparations.

"'Morning, girls," Jack said cheerfully as he entered.

"Good morning, Jen said. She was determined to be polite.

Josie did not answer.

"Good morning Josie," there was a steely pitch to Jack's tone that had Jen looking from one to the other in surprise.

Josie mumbled something but did not turn to look at Jack. He in turn ignored her. He basically ignored Jen also, leaving Jen even more confused. She took covert glances at him throughout breakfast, but he seemed preoccupied. Clearly, he was going to work, and she assumed that was the reason he had lifted her grounding.

"When they were about finished the silence and uncomfortable breakfast, Jen stood up. "I study better at school so I'm going there today, she announced.

Josie did not look up. Uncle Jack barely glanced at her before resuming his meal. Neither one answered. Jen shrugged and left the room. She really wanted to go by Richard's job, but it was too early, besides she decided she would go into school first, just in case Uncle Jack continued checking up on her. Jen did not have Rita's schedule, but with freedom from Josie spying, she could now question students in Rita's form.

Neither Rita nor Monique were at school, however Jen found out that Rita would be there the next day. By midday she was on the bus to downtown Kingston, hoping to catch Richard at lunch. This time she was determined to explain more of her life.

"Where to?" Richard asked. They were walking, hand linked away from his office building.

"The park?"

He nodded. They stopped at a shop for lunch.

"Two patties an' coco-bread please," Richard called out. Coco-bread is commonly paired the Jamaican patty. It is a sweet and starchy bread made with coconut milk. To eat with the patty, it is cut in half and the patty placed between the two halves to form a sandwich. He also ordered half pint of orange joint for himself and a half pint of cherry milk for Jen.

"Do you remember when I got upset when you and Rita were singing the song '*Brown girl in the ring*?" Jen asked. They were sitting side-by-side on a low wall surrounding one of the memorials.

Richard gave puzzled look but nodded, "Sure."

Jen took a bite of her patty and coco-bread and chewed slowly as she looked up. From where she was sitting, she could just see the clock tower of Kingston Parish Church. They had toured the cemetery attached to the church and found graves dating back to 1699. "I was thirteen before I looked it up and got the words right."

"What do you mean?"

"When I was little, I loved to sing that song, but I didn't have the right words. I used to sing, "*And she likes sugar, and I like plum*," but the actual verse is "*She looks like a sugar in a plum*."

"I've done that," his tone was noncommittal, and Jen imaged he was trying to figure out what she was getting at. Yet she knew he wouldn't rush her. She loved that about him.

"Dad used to take us on lots of trips when we were small."

"Trips to where?"

"All over the island. You know. Tourist spots. He felt we should know our country."

"Neat idea. I want to do that. I've never explored Jamaica. Maybe we can plan something."

Jen gave a faint smile. "Monique wants to invite us to Cayman Island. Did Rita tell you?"

"I heard. Are you interested?"

She looked anxiously over at him. "You would

go…? With me?"

He nodded, smiled and reached across the food to squeeze her hand. "Let's talk about that some other time."

She took a deep breath. "Josie and I were quarrelling the night my parent died. I can't forgive myself."

"Quarrelling about what?"

Slowly, Jen begin telling him about the accident that killed her parent. Halfway through the tale, Richard scooped up their lunch and scooted over to her side. He pulled her closer as he placed their unfinished lunch behind Jen.

"I felt it was my fault," Jen concluded.

"It was an accident." Richard insisted. "The other driver should have been charged with reckless driving. I know that road. There is no space to pass, so even if he was watching the road like a hawk your father would not have had many options."

Jen said nothing. She hugged him tightly. She still felt she was at fault. But she was now sensible enough to recognize that she could not change the past.

For a few minutes they stay tightly together, then Richard jostled her gently. "Were you just afraid to talk to anyone?"

"I don't know. Maybe… I remember wanting to keep Josie happy. I was afraid she would die too. I stayed with her while she was in the hospital….It was awful. She wasn't interested in anything." Jen stopped for a minute. "At first she was so….. it was like she didn't care if she died. I was just terrified she would leave me too. Letting her tell me what to do helped her. I was afraid I would say the wrong thing… afraid she wouldn't get better… I was just terrified. So, I started letting her answer questions for me…. " Again, Jen paused. Richard said nothing and after a minute she continued. "She so loved managing me…. I think it helped her cope. So, I let her do it. It was easier for me too. Besides I didn't really want to talk to anyone. I felt so guilty about everything…."

"Do you think your parents would have blamed you?" Richard finally asked.

Jen was silent for a moment. She then slowly shook her head. "I guess not." She rested her head on his chest. "I'm messed up."

"Didn't you tell your Aunt anything?"

She hesitated. "I got the impression… maybe I was wrong."

"What?"

"I don't think she really cared. She was our only close relative. It would have looked bad if she didn't take us…." Her voice trailed off. "Anyway, after…after …. I got it in my head that one wrong word could get someone killed. It was better to keep my mouth shut. So, I was afraid to say anything. Then… Josie liked it better if she did all the talking. She would get annoyed if I said anything. I wanted to keep her happy…It became a habit I guess."

"Uumm."

"I tried to change later but by then it was too late. It was too hard…. I didn't want to hurt her feelings. I don't know. I was comfortable remaining unnoticed and was afraid people would expect me to be talkative and outgoing like Josie. I guess I didn't want to be bothered. I should have to talk to people…." She sighed.

"You were being silly."

Jen sniffed.

"You are not going to cry on me are you," he asked

suspiciously.

"No," but she sniffed again.

"This is my good shirt," he said teasingly. "And I have to go back to work. If you are going to cry let me know so I can take it off."

She pulled back to give him a playful thump on the chest with her fist. Then looked up.

Richard was smiling at her. "I'm glad you finally decided to be bothered and joined the real world."

"Me too." She smiled, then frowned. "I just wish…" she stopped.

Richard did not prompt her, and she finally continued. "I wished Josie hadn't started… I wish I didn't find out…" again she stopped.

This time Richard competed… "that you twin is seeing a married man."

Jen sighed again. "I don't understand her now."

"You are twins, but you are two separate people. You can't live her life for her Jen. She has to make her own decisions, her own mistakes."

"It's not just because I'm her twin that I feel this way. I think I would feel like this for any brother or sister. I can't just leave her to mess up her life. I have to try to help her."

"Is she listening to you?"

Jen looked down. "I don't know what to do?"

"Leave her alone."

She sighed again.

"Come on, Jen." Richard lifted her chin. "I know that your sister has problems. But you've tried and you just admitted that there is nothing much more you can do to. Let's concentrate on us for a while."

"Ok," she agreed quietly.

Josie was depressed again. Jen tried not to care but she was worried. Next week was Physics, their final exam. Despite their differences when she got home on Friday she planned on talking to Josie again.

Josie would not see her, however. Jen tried calling and knocking on the door. No answer. She knew she was in there. After a few more minute of trying Jen finally gave up and went to her room.

She fixed dinner and later that evening she was the only one in the dining room when Uncle Jack came in.

He was furious.

"Where is Josie?"

"She's in her room,"

Uncle Jack was so mad that, despite the fact the Aunt Beryl was sleeping in her room he immediately began shouting.

"Josie! Josie!"

Jen stayed where she was. Uncle Jack was now rapping sharply on Josie's room door.

"Open the door, Josie. I know you are in there."

Josie had been simply lying on the bed staring into space. She reluctantly got up and opened the door. She faced a furious Jack.

He stormed in slamming the door swearing. "Why didn't you show up!" he demanded.

"I told you I wasn't going to." Josie avoided his eyes, and seemed, outwardly at least, to be calm.

"You listen to me, and you listen good." Jack grabbed her by both shoulders. Josie's projected calm had merely irritated him further. "I'm going to make another appointment," he shook her to emphasize his point. "You heard me!" he didn't wait for an answer, "and this time you are going to keep it." He lowered his voice. "You hear me Josie."

Josie started crying. "Jack it's starting to show. I can't...."

He slapped her face.

"Jack...?" she wailed, holding her face and staring up at him in shock.

"Shut up!"

Josie bent her head, crying.

Jack wiped his hand across his mouth as he took a turn about the room and wondered what to do.

He swore to himself. Who would believe Josie could be so stubborn?

"Listen Josie." he said harshly. "There is no way on earth you are going to force me to mind you and that baby."

Josie still had her head bent. She began sniffing. "You don't have to mind us. I'll find a way to look after the baby."

"How? By begging on the streets." he gave a short laugh.

He could see now that Jen would never turn to him. He didn't want Josie to have the baby, period! No way was he going to mess up his marriage. Her Aunt Beryl didn't know about any of his numerous affairs, and he wanted to keep it that way. He had briefly considered sending Josie away—perhaps to another parish—in return for her silence. But after thinking it out he realized that would not work. There was Jen to consider. Besides, sooner or later the truth would come out. Jen for instance might guess that he was the father of the baby, or Josie would tell her.

"I'm going to make another appointment for next Thursday. This time you stay here and I'll come and pick you up; and I am warning you, you mess this up...." he paused leaving the sentence unfinished. "You got that."

Josie nodded.

He slammed out of the room.

Josie threw herself on the bed crying in earnest. What should she do? She had believed Jack's promises. In fact, she still could not believe he had changed his mind about the baby and was even now hoping he would change it back. She had missed the appointment thinking that he would relent if he found out that she was determined to keep the baby. Now she didn't know what to do. They had no close relatives that she could turn to. She couldn't tell Jen; there wasn't much that Jen could do anyway, besides she was beginning to get afraid of Jack and what he would do if she confided in her twin. She cried even harder. Jack didn't love her! She wished she were dead.

Jack passed Jen in the kitchen without speaking. She had heard the shouting, and as indistinct as it was, there could be no mistaking Uncle Jack's anger. What on earth was going on? She softly crossed the corridor to Josie's room. She listened at the door for a moment. Josie was crying. Jen tried the door. It opened.

"Josie?" Jen questioned softly.

Josie did not turn around although she must have heard the door opening. She continued crying as Jen approached her bed.

Jen sat down beside her and patted her back. "Josie,

please tell me what's wrong."

Josie turned around and reached for her twin. The two hugged tightly. "Everything is so messed up. I don't know what to do," Josie finally said wearily.

"But what happened? Why's Uncle Jack so mad? Did you tell him that you don't want him anymore? Is that why he's so mad?"

Josie buried her face in Jen's shoulder. She was still sniffing and hic-cupping. Jen gently stroked her hair.

"I can't tell you."

"Josie! Crying like this won't help. You know I won't tell anyone if you don't want me to, and maybe I can help."

"I'm pregnant," Josie baldly admitted.

Jen's hands stilled. She was silent for a minute. "Is that why Uncle Jack is so angry?"

"Last week he told me it was ok. But then he changed his mind. He doesn't want me to have the baby. He made the appointment for today and I didn't show up. I couldn't."

"So, what will we do now?"

Jen had automatically included herself in her twin's plans. For that Josie squeezed her tightly. "He has made another appointment, for Thursday."

"Are you going to do it?"

Josie sighed, "I don't know what to do."

"Listen Josie. You have met Rita, right." at Josie's slight nod she continued, "Well, her mother is awfully nice. Maybe she can help."

"No!" Josie leaned away from Jen's shoulders. "Promise me you won't tell anyone."

Jen hesitated.

"You must promise me Jen," Josie insisted.

"All right," she agreed. "But I still think she would be able to help."

"I don't want anyone knowing."

"They will soon know once the baby start showing," Jen pointed out.

"Not if…. I could go away, somewhere."

Jen thought for a minute then said. "Do you remember that there was a trust fund set up for us?" Josie nodded. "Well, we are eighteen soon, maybe we can use some of the money. I could find out from Aunt Beryl."

"Oh, Jen! That's it!" Josie was excited. "We could take the money and go to the country. We could live together and maybe you could get a job since I will have to stay home and look after the baby. When the baby is older, we could come back I could even say I got married and my husband left me."

"Come on Josie, nobody will believe that," Jen objected.

"Well, I don't really care what people want to think, as long as they don't know the truth. I want this baby." She gave a hic-cup laugh. "I still love him. Even though he doesn't love me. This baby will let me keep a part of him. And maybe he will regret leaving me and come back."

Jen did not comment. She did not see that happening. Uncle Jack did not strike her as a caring man. Maybe she was bias, but she could not stand him. But she was not about to start an argument with her twin.

"Will you find out from Aunt Beryl tomorrow?" Josie asked anxiously.

"Ok, I will. Are you sure you're alright now?"

"Yes, I am ok, remember that you promised not to tell anyone. Don't even let Jack know that you know."

"I won't."

The two hugged again. Jen felt good. At least she had her twin back and they were communicating again.

"What about Physics, Josie?" she asked drawing away again.

"I don't know. I guess I have been too worried to study."

"Well, there is not much time left."

"I know, I know. I am going to try."

"Rita and Monique are meeting me at school Monday. Do you want to come?"

"No. I don't feel like studying with a group; besides I don't want anyone suspecting anything. I think I am getting bigger. I'll study at home."

Jen did not think anyone would know of her pregnancy. Josie was very small. But to keep the tentative peace she agreed. "Ok, but you have to promise that you will study, especially since you are having the baby. You have to pass something. Remember you will have to find a job afterwards."

"I promise, I'll study. Satisfied." Josie was grinning, cheerful now.

Jen grinned back. "Later then. I'm going to check on dinner." She left the room.

As Jen left, she realized that neither of them had considered what Uncle Jack's reaction would be when he heard of the change of plans. She debated whether to say anything to Josie then decided to leave it for now. She would find out about the money first.

Dinner was another uneasy meal. Josie was subdued, and Uncle Jack broody. The atmosphere gave Jen a distinct feeling of disquiet. The only consolation was that

Uncle Jack didn't bother questioning her. She left the table as soon as she possibly could and was not surprised when Josie left almost immediately afterwards. Instinctively, they had decided not to let Uncle Jack know that they had made up.

Jen was unable to get Aunt Beryl alone to speak to her during the weekend. Uncle Jack was there the entire weekend or if he was out, then so too was Aunt Beryl. After a brief word with Josie, they decided that the best time would probably the following Monday before Uncle Jack got in from work. Since nothing was settled, she was still a bit worried and wondered if she should say anything to Richard. She had not seen him since Friday but if she were to go away with Josie what would happen to them?

Would Richard wait for her to return? Would he need to get an explanation? She had promised Josie not to say anything, but she couldn't just leave. What on earth was she going to tell him?

That Monday she met Rita and Monique at school. Of course, the biggest discussion was the proposed trip to Cayman Islands.

"I say we go right after the exams," Rita suggested.

"Are you going with Jason?" Jen asked.

"What's wrong with Jason," Rita defensively.

"Nothing is wrong with him. It's just that you two are always arguing."

"Mike agrees with me on everything," Monique pointed out. "I don't have to argue with him."

Jen wasn't sure that relationship was much better. But who was she to throw stones?

Rita was scowling at them both. "I like Jason," she

declared.

Jen held up her hand in surrender, "So do I."

"I like Mike better," Monique inserted.

"That's why he is your boyfriend not mine."

"Let's see which dates would be best for us?" Jen said hurriedly. She was wondering if the trip was such a good idea. Monique had been getting on Rita's nerves lately and Jason and Rita were always arguing….

Later, when she met Richard for lunch, she told him details of the planned trip.

"It will be great… if we don't all murder each other," he commented.

"We don't have to go everywhere with them."

"Separate room?"

"Two rooms. One for us girls and one for you guys."

He grinned. "I'm not happy but I can deal. A large hotel on the beachfront has lots of possibilities."

Jen felt her cheeks heat.

His grin widened and with a laugh he bent and kissed her on the nose. Embarrassed Jen ducked her head and focused on her sandwich. Richard's arms came around her, pulling her to his side.

"Richard?" she began hesitantly, reluctant to bring up a negative topic but recognizing that she had to.

"Um'um," his mouth was in her hair.

Feeling a bit braver she began running her hand up and down his back. Maybe she would tell him some other time, she thought.

"Something's on your mind." Richard was now kissing her ears. "Tell me."

"I may have to leave Kingston for a while," she got

out in a rush.

Richard put her away from him. "Leave? And go where?" he was clearly puzzled.

Jen hugged herself, suddenly feeling deprived of his warmth. She was unable to meet his eyes as she began her explanation. "Well... I... I may have to go to the country. What I mean is....we..." she stopped to look pleadingly up at him.

He considered her for a minute, then pulled her in a hug again. This time he stroked her head. Jen relaxed.

"Is your twin pregnant?" he asked quietly, abruptly.

Jen tried to jerk away, but Richard held her firmly. She finally gave up and relaxed again. "Who told you?" she asked, resigned.

"No one told me anything."

"So how did you know?"

"I know that your twin has been acting odd lately, and that you were worried stiff. Now you are both planning to go away. It was an educated guess."

He paused, then asked curiously, "Does Rita know that she is pregnant?"

"No, but I told her ...." Jen hesitated, then continued, "I told her that Josie was seeing a married man."

"And it's his child?"

"Yes."

Richard rubbed his jaws. "What a mess! What about the man? Does he know, or doesn't he care?"

"He knows but... well... "

"He doesn't want to have anything to do with her now. Right."

"He wants her to have an abortion, and she doesn't want to," Jen muttered.

"It probably would be for the best."

"Richard! How can you say that?"

"Come on Jen, get real. Your twin is seventeen; she hasn't completed her education; she has no job. She can't even take care of herself, much less a child. She probably hasn't even thought about it. Caring for the child when it comes, I mean."

"I don't know." Jen shifted uncomfortably; she hadn't thought about baby care either.

"Does your aunt agree with all this?"

Jen didn't answer.

He pulled her away from his chest. "You haven't told her, have you?"

"Josie doesn't want anyone to know."

Richard shook his head, incredulously. "Be sensible Jen, there is no way your aunt is not going to find out. On an island this size? You've got to be kidding. Someone who knows both you and your aunt or uncle is bound to find out and eventually tell her, no matter where you live. And who were you planning on staying with, then?"

"I don't know." Jen raised anxious eyes to meet his expression of utter disbelief. "We haven't really planned it out as yet," she added lamely.

Richard stood up. He couldn't believe what he was hearing. Rubbing the back of his neck he slowly paced in front of the ledge. "I need to get this straight. Josie is pregnant. Right?"

Jen nodded.

"The baby father is married and wants nothing to do with her or the child."

When Jen just bit her lips he continued, "And your

aunt and uncle know nothing about this. So, what were you planning on telling them?"

Jen concentrated on smoothing out a crease in her skirt. "Well you see, there was a trust set up for us after our parents died. We were just going to move out after the exams and use the money to board somewhere. We hadn't really thought out what to tell her as yet."

"But don't you have any other relatives?"

"No. Not really. At least not anyone close. Our mother was an only child and our father had only one sister. I remember meeting some cousins years ago, but we really haven't kept in touch, and I don't know where they are now."

"Listen Jen, your plan stinks. I am telling you, it's not going to work, take it from me. I suggest you go home and have a good talk with your twin and your aunt. Talk your twin out of going away or better yet talk her into having the abortion. Whatever you or your twin decide, you have to tell your aunt."

Jen shook her head helplessly, "I can't Richard. It's a lot more complicated than just the pregnancy. I can't explain. I shouldn't even have told you all this. I promised Josie that I wouldn't tell anyone."

Richard gave up, he lifted his head. The sky was clouding over. "Come, we'd better go, it's getting late, and I have to get back to work, besides it looks like it's going to rain." He waited only long enough to make sure that she had actually gotten up from the ledge before starting on a brisk walk towards the park's exit.

Jen hurried to keep up with him. "Richard," she appealed, "Josie is determined to go and I can't let her go by herself."

"Two fools is not better than one," was his sarcastic response.

Jen bit her lips. There was no further communication between them until they reached the exit. There Richard stopped so suddenly that Jen, who had never quite caught up with him, stumbled and bumped into his back.

He turned and steadied her. "So, when will you be leaving?"

Jen looked warily up at him. "I still have one physic exam left. Wednesday of this week. After that, I imagine."

"Well, I suppose I should give thanks that you have the sense to complete your exams," he commented nastily.

Jen felt depressed. "You don't understand."

"What is there to understand," his voice was filled with frustrated anger, "It's a dumb fool idea and it won't work, especially if the idea is for no one to know that Josie is pregnant. Listen, let's not talk about it anymore, or I may just say something we'll both regret." He paused, then asked politely, "Bye the way, were you planning on returning to Kingston or going to college?"

"I guess so." Jen was uncertain.

Richard did not comment on her response. "Come on, I have to get back to work. We have to hurry. I'll follow you to the bus stop."

Richard was silent on the way to the bus stop and after glancing at his frowning face Jen could not work up the courage to start a conversation. She could even understand his frustration. She just couldn't do anything about it. While she could understand Richards point, she simply didn't see how they could change their plans. They had to leave.

"You'll let me know what happens, won't you?" he

asked quietly.

Jen nodded, then gathered her courage to ask. "Do you still want to see me?"

"Probably," Richard sighed, then at her worried look he continued, "Stop looking so worried. I'll always want to see you. We'll meet after your exam on Wednesday. Is it in the morning?"

"Yes. 9 o'clock."

"Good. So, meet at my workplace for lunch after."

Jen nodded as she gave him a tentative smile.

"Just don't leave without telling me, and make sure you let me know where you're going, Ok?"

"I will," Jen was relieved, she smiled widened.

He gave her a rueful grin in return, then pulled her gently towards him and kissed her briefly on the lips. "Your plan still stinks," he whispered as he released her."

"I'll try talking to Josie," Jen promised.

"Good. Bye now,"

Jen waved as the parted.

Uncle Jack and Aunt Beryl were not home when Jen got back. They learned that Aunt Beryl was not going to work, and Uncle Jack had got in early and had taken her out. Jen went into Josie's room and the two sat on her bed, chatting. Jen was trying to think of another alternative to going away but was unable to come up with anything the satisfied Josie. She finally remembered Uncle Jack.

"Bye the way Josie, what is going to happen on Thursday."

"Thursday?" Josie had forgotten all about the doctor's appointment that Jack had made. Jen reminded her. "Oh, Aunt Beryl will be here, he can't force me to go with him."

"But what will he do. I mean, he will be furious."

"There is not much he can do," Josie said with airy confidence. "After all it's my child too. If he gets nasty, I will just threaten to tell Aunt Beryl."

"I thought you didn't want her to know."

"He doesn't know that."

Jen chewed worriedly at her lips. "I'll stay home on Thursday too, just in case. Ok."

A car drove up the driveway.

"Josie got off the bed to look out the window. "It's them," she announced.

Jen got up as well. "I had better go, and you had better take up your book Josie."

"I will. See you later."

Jen spent some time helping Aunt Beryl fix dinner and tidy up the house. They had a helper who came in once a week, usually on Friday, to clean and dust. However, whenever Aunt Beryl was home, she insisted that the house needed another `going over' as she put it. Josie got out of helping by pleading a headache and Jen, remembering her pregnancy, backed up her story.

With Aunt Beryl there, at least the atmosphere at dinner was not as strained, as before. Knowing that they had only a one-day grace period–Aunt Beryl would be back at work tomorrow—Jen made the most of it. Afterwards she sat in the living room and watched an episode of the comedy soap opera, Lime Tree Lane. She hadn't watched any television in a while, since she didn't want to sit with Josie and Uncle Jack or even worse, Uncle Jack alone. Fortunately, it was a very popular show and she had heard, often times blow-by-blow descriptions, of past episodes from the girls at school so it was easy to figure out what was going on.

Josie didn't stay. She went back to her room immediately after dinner, and Uncle Jack after pretending and interest in the program finally gave up and disappeared in the study. After he left, Jen glanced up at her aunt wondering if she should begin questioning her now.

Aunt Beryl was busy with her knitting. She was making a sweater and looked up enquiringly at Jen. "Something wrong Jen?"

"No. No," Jen said hurriedly, deciding that it was too risky. Uncle Jack might hear, or he may decide to come back in the room just as she got started.

"How are your studies coming along?"

"Fine so far, Aunt Beryl. I only have one subject left."

"Good. Good." Aunt Beryl went back to her knitting.

After the program, Jen decided that she might as well get on with her studies. She could not focus on the television anyway.

Tuesday–throughout the day–was uneventful. Uncle Jack was at work, so even Josie began looking cheerful, although she didn't want to leave her room. Jen suspected she was afraid Aunt Beryl would comment on her increasing size. She tried telling her twin that her pregnancy was almost impossible to detect but Josie was not convinced. Jen decided not to tempt fate by disappearing two days in a row, so stayed in and studied most of the day. Aunt Beryl went to bed immediately after dinner. She had to work that night and needed her sleep. Uncle Jack went out again. Jen assumed that he told his wife where he was going, he certainly didn't mention it to either of the two girls, anyway with him gone and Aunt Beryl asleep, Josie emerged from her room. The two of them played one or two card games and watched the television until they heard Uncle Jack's car pulling up in the driveway. Jen looked at the clock. It was almost ten o'clock.

"Aunt Beryl will be up soon." she commented.

Josie got up and stretched. "I'm for bed. Besides I don't want to see him for tonight again." she said meaning Jack.

Jen nodded, "Me neither." she muttered, as they left for their respective rooms.

It was sometime later that night that Jen woke to a hand gently shaking her shoulder.

"Hu'um," she muttered turning.

"Jen! Jen!" someone whispered.

Jen's eyes flew open. Uncle Jack was bending over her. He was fully clothed and for a moment she thought something disastrous had happened.

"What is it? What's wrong?"

"Shush!" he whispered.

Now fearful, Jen sat up, dragging the light sheet covering with her. "What are you doing in my room? How did you get in?" She knew that she had locked the door.

Jack dangled a set of keys in front of her face. "The spare keys. From your aunt's rooms," he sat on the bed.

"If you don't get out, I'll scream," Jen warned. She wondered if he were drunk. His breath stank of beer.

"Come Jen, I don't want to hurt you. Just give me a kiss and I'll leave," he leaned over her.

"You're drunk. Get out of my room," Jen said,

scrambling to the other side of the bed.

"Not drunk, just happy," Jack grinned, "Come on just one little kiss. You know how much I love you."

Jen eyed the door. Would she be able to get around the bed and get out?

"I'm warning you; I'll scream if you don't leave me alone."

"Scream all you like. Your aunt's not here and Josie is asleep."

Jen scrambled off the bed on the other side and tried to make it to the door. Jack lunged across the bed, grabbing her around the waist. Jen started to scream, but he clamped a hand over her mouth. She bit down, hard.

"Ouch! You bitch!" He released her momentarily only to slap her face. Jen was stunned. Before she could recover, he had dragged her onto the bed. He stuffed one end of the pillowcase into her mouth and held it in place.

"Let's see you bite me through that." He gave a grunt of satisfaction, and then pressed his full body on top of her. His weight effectively kept her immobilized on the bed.

Jen began struggling in earnest as he ripped her night dress. She scratched at his face forcing him to release her mouth. He grabbed hold of both of her hands with his left hand and used his right to slap her repeatedly across the face.

Wham. Wham. Left side. Right side. The blows rained on.

"Shut up! Shut up!"

Jen face was stinging. She was weak and confused when he paused… and he was not done yet….

Chapter 15

Jen was quiet now, but tears were streaming down her face. She averted her face.

"Listen, honey, I'm sorry," he attempted to wipe her face with the pillowcase, but Jen jerked her face away. "Look I didn't mean this to happen. Not like this. If you hadn't struggled so hard none of this would have happened...."

Was he actually blaming her? Jen thought hysterically.

"...The next time it won't be so bad. I'll go slowly...."

His voice drone on, but by them Jen had stopped listening. Was he mad! Did he actually believe she would let him do this to her again? After a bit he stopped talking and waited awhile. Since she hadn't been listening and refused to look at him. Jen wasn't sure what he was waiting for. She didn't even know whether he had asked a question or not. Her mind was blank, all she wanted was for him to get out and leave her alone. He finally gave a heaving sigh, got off the bed.

Her body stiffened in rejection as he bent over her again, but he merely pulled the light sheet covering up to her chin and said, "I'll make up. I didn't mean this to happen Jen. I really love you. I'll get you something. Ok. See you tomorrow."

Jen lay perfectly still as he left the room, closing the

door softly behind him. For a long time, she just lay there, crying. First, she blamed Josie, she just felt that if Josie hadn't started none of this would have happened, then she realized her reasoning was absurd. She had no one to blame but herself. She should never have kept Josie's secret. She was an idiot. This was her fault.

After a while her crying subsided to occasional hiccups. She listened carefully. The house was completely silent. Uncle Jack's tone had expressed his confidence that he would continue using her. No way was Jen going to allow that to happen. She was not Josie. She slowly got up. Her night dress was torn; she didn't want to put it back on. She threw it to floor and draped the sheet about her body. She then crept out of the room, stopping again to listen. Silence. There was no light on in the house, that she could see.

She quickly went into the bathroom, closed and locked the door. After dropping the sheet, she got into the bathtub and turned on the cold shower. First, she soaped her entire body, then she scrubbed of vigorously. Not an inch of her body was spared. She even washed her hair. She soaped and washed off twice before she was finally satisfied that she could become no cleaner. It took a few more minutes for her to step out of the shower and dry off. She then realized that she hadn't brought any clean clothes with her. She eyed the bed sheet with distaste. There were splotches of blood on it. Nothing on earth would get her to put it near her body again. She wrapped the towel about her body and secured it under her armpit. Opening the bathroom door, she paused and listened. Nothing. Just as silently, she reentered her room. She got dressed, quickly, automatically, then hurriedly combed and braided her wet hair. It wasn't until she was ready that she realized that without even thinking about it she had decided to leave.

Now! Tonight! She would go to Rita's home. She wasn't even going to wake Josie. Josie would try to talk her out of leaving.

She stuffed a few of her personal belongings in a bag—a comb, her toothbrush, a change of underwear, a dress and a few more pieces of clothing. She then took one last glance about the room, before hurrying out. She stopped in the corridor to listen again. Still nothing. Nevertheless, just to be safe, she decided to use the back door. Uncle Jack slept in the front bedroom in the opposite wing of the house, she didn't want to take the chance of waking him. Without turning on the lights, she silently traversed the living and dining rooms, the kitchen and finally the washroom. Her heart was literally pounding by the time she got to the back door. She fumbled with the locks, before finally opening the door. Breathing a sigh of relief, she slipped out.

It was a dark night. The moon was obscured by cloud and only a few stars, through a heroic effort, were able to shine their way through. Jen looked up; she took a deep reviving breath. It was a beautiful night. She thought of the first time Richard had walk her home. She closed her eyes, but the tears made their way down nevertheless. She sniffed and rubbed her eyes with the back of her hands. Her thoughts however had started another flood of tear. She covered her face with both hands and wept again. She sank slowly to the ground, and remained there, hunched over, her bag resting on the grass at her feet.

It was a while before she became aware of the sounds of the night, and the night was alive with sounds, both of nature and of man. At this hour there was little or no traffic on the streets, but, because of this lack, rumbling of the occasional car, truck or van sounded abnormally loud. It shook the ground, signaling the approach of the vehicle and with the rumbles continuing even after the vehicle had passed. Then there were the dogs: It seemed as if they had chosen the night to carry on their lengthiest conversations. Bark followed bark, sometimes rising to a crescendo of yap and howls only to subside then start all over again in a song she was incapable of understanding. And of course, the insects had to put in their little bit. The crickets in particular seemed to be competing for the loudest cricket award.

The sounds had a curiously calming effect on Jen. For a while she just sat there, on the ground with her eyes closed and allowed the sounds to wash over her. Finally, she opened her eyes and looked up. It was still peaceful, but it was also beginning to feel chilly, and her wet hair had soaked through her clothing at the back. Jen looked down at her watch.

Two o'clock. She paused. She hadn't realized it was so late, or rather so early. Standing up she circled the house and went to the front gate. She couldn't go back, so she might as well go forward. Opening the gate, she went out. By half-running and half-walking, it was close to two-thirty before she breathlessly opened the gate of Rita's home. She went up the small walkway to the front door and started knocking.

It seemed like hours but was probably only a few minutes later that she saw lights coming on in the house. Finally, a voice, Richard's voice called out:

"Who is it?"

"Me, Jen."

"Jen!"

Jen heard other exclamation in the background and guessed that Rita and her mother were up as well. There were the sounds of the door being opened. Finally, Richard appeared, he had on shorts and nothing else. Uncle Jack had worn clothes yet for some reason Richard's bare chest immediately reminded Jen of what she had just endured.

"Jen what on earth are you doing here at this hour? What's wrong?"

Jen couldn't answer. She stepped back as he stepped toward her and avoided looking at his eyes. She was fighting to hold back tears.

Ms. Taylor pushed pass her son. "Let's not start an inquisition here at the door. Come on in Jen." She noted the two bags that Jen was carrying. "Richard, take her bags will you."

Richard moved to take Jen bags.

"It's okay," she clutched them to her body. "They're not heavy."

Richard dropped his outstretched hand and looked over at his mother for further instructions. Ms. Taylor did not try to persuade Jen to hand over her bags, with flicking motions of her head she indicated to Richard and Rita that she wanted them out of the way. Neither of her children demurred. They were as mystified as their mother as to why Jen should choose to come here in the middle of the night. Such an action indicated something serious, so Richard was frowning as he left the room. Rita, silent, had spent the entire time staring at Jen. By mutual agreement the two retired to Richard's room.

It was obviously a man's room and furnished in a purely functional manner. A double-bed, complete with a bookcase-headboard and a trunk, attached at the foot of the bed, dominated the room. A student desk, a chair and a bookcase took up just about all the space to the right of the door, which left a narrow passage, to the left of the door and sandwiched between the bed and the wall, for the wardrobe.

"What do you suppose happened," Rita had recovered her voice. She took a seat on the chair and now sat facing Richard who was seated on the bed trunk.

Richard shook his head, "I don't know." He was staring absently at the floor, his brows still furrowed in a frown.

"Maybe she and her twin had a fight."

"She would hardly come rushing here at three in the morning over some silly fight."

"I was just kidding," Rita teased.

"Well, this isn't something to kid about," Richard gave Rita a hard stare, before jumping to his feet. He began pacing in the confined space, "Something must be terribly wrong."

Rita stared at him. What was his problem? She opened her mouth to say something, then slowly closed it again. This was the first time she had ever seen her brother upset over a girl. Even when they left him, and a few had, he would just shrug it off, with a comment like, 'Plenty more fish in the pond.' Now she wasn't sure what was going on. Was he serious about Jen?

"What's taking them so long?" Richard ran his hands distractedly through his hair.

After a while, it seemed like hours to Rita, but the clock on the wall showed that only fifteen minutes had passed, Richard stopped his pacing and turned to her. He gave her a wry glance on noting her questing look.

"You really like her," she confirmed.

"Yeah," he admitted.

"You do? Just yesterday you denied it."

He shrugged staring at the ground, "Just leave it, ok."

"But why the big secret?"

He gave her an ironic look, "Come on Rita, think. You know what you're like when you know the girl I am interested in seeing. I get teased to death, and so does the poor girl."

"Does Jen feel the same about you?"

"Rita can we not have this conversation now?"

Rita scowled at him.

He grinned faintly them frowned again.

"What do you think happened?' she asked.

Richard shook his head. "She was okay when I last saw her. Although...," his voice trailed off. Could this have anything to do with what she had told him of her plans to leave Kingston?

"Although what?" Rita asked impatiently when he didn't complete the sentence.

Richard shook his head slightly. He resumed his pacing, his frown deepening. From past experience, Rita knew that she would get nothing further from him.

She looked down over at a wall clock. Jen's explanation was taking a long time! Ignoring Richard, she went to the bedroom door,

"Where are you going?" he immediately demanded, looking up.

"Nowhere. I was just wondering whether they were still talking or not." Rita peeked out the door. She could hear the mummer of her mother's voice but little else, without going into the corridor.

"Are they still talking?" Richard was right behind her.

Rita nodded. "Yes, but I can't hear anything." Then, "Shh... Mom is coming."

They both scrambled away from the door.

Rita was again seated on the chair, but Richard was still standing when their mother entered the room.

"What's wrong Mom?" Richard asked, coming towards her.

Ms. Taylor was wearing a deep frown. "Sit down, sit down," she said to Richard as he approached her.

He sat on the bed, reluctantly.

"So, what's wrong," he repeated.

Ms. Taylor rubbed her hands together. "This is very serious. I'll explain as soon as Jen gets settled in for tonight. She will be staying here by-the-way."

"But..." Richard began.

"Later, Richard, later. First, I am going to close this door and put Jen in my room for tonight. She doesn't feel up to seeing anyone right now. Is there anything that you think you will need Rita?"

Rita shook her head, "Not for tonight. No."

"Good. Maybe you can open the folding cot and put it in the dining room for the rest of the night."

"But where will you sleep?" This from Rita.

"I'm going to stay with her tonight. I know this is going to be a bit confusing, but it really is terrible what has happened and there really is not much we can do at this hour."

"Oh, I don't mind," Rita reassured her.

"Good, good," still frowning Ms. Taylor left the

room, closing the door quietly behind her.

Richard and Rita exchanged worried glances. Neither said anything. There was silence as they both listened to the sounds of their mother's voice outside the room, and the softer sounds coming from Jen. After a bit there no more sounds to be heard. Their mother had entered her bedroom and closed the door. Richard began pacing the room again. He finally stopped beside the window, the one on the opposite wall, facing the wardrobe. He leaned against the wall and crossed on leg over the other, then folded his arms across his chest. He stared outside. Rita couldn't imagine what he was staring at. It was still dark outside. She really liked Jen. She hadn't dared hope that her brother was serious, however.

It was a good twenty minutes before Ms. Taylor returned. Rita had spent the time flicking through a magazine and Richard had not budged from the window. They had not exchanged a single word.

Their mother rapped on the door before entering. They both looked to her expectantly. Ms. Taylor smoothed back her hair with her hands as she shook her head sadly. She sat down on the bed trunk and began.

"It's a longish story...." Briefly she told them everything that Jen had told her, finishing with, "Jen gave me her permission to tell you both everything. She also wants to stay here. This is where it gets complicated. You see, she doesn't want to press any charges against her uncle, but she wants her sister and her aunt to know what he did."

As her mother paused, Rita closed her mouth. She hadn't even realized that she had had it open. She looked across at Richard. His face was blank. He had been listening intently as his mother talked, he now turned back to stare out the window.

Rita cleared her throat, "So did you tell her that she can stay here."

"Yes, I did—at least for now. I know that we really don't have the space and will be cramped, but I don't see what else I could have suggested. As you can imagine she is terribly hurt and upset, and they have no close relatives..."

"I will move out," Richard spoke up suddenly.

"What?" his mother asked.

Without turning around, he explained, "I have a friend whose mother takes boarder. I will go and live there."

"No Richard. I can't have Jen driving you out of your own house. Perhaps we can work something else out. Maybe Jen could even stay there, at your friend's mother's place."

"She's not driving me out Mom. I was thinking of leaving anyway. I want to be closer to work," Richard had turned around to emphasize his point. "Besides I hardly think she would be comfortable living with total strangers."

"That is beside the point," his mother objected.

They continued arguing the point until Ms. Taylor at last agreed, after Richard insisted, he would leave anyway. She was not happy though.

"Come on Mom. I am not going to the ends of the earth," Richard chided her. "What will you say if or when I leave for America?"

"This is different, and you know it. You would never even have considered leaving here if Jen hadn't asked if she could stay."

"Who knows?" Richard refused to concede.

"What about Jen's things Mom," Rita had been

silent while they had been arguing.

"Oh. That's another thing," Ms. Taylor turned back to her son. "Could you come with me tomorrow to the aunt's house? I have to speak with her. I also promised Jen that I would collect her things."

Richard grimaced, but nodded.

"What about Josie?" Rita asked.

Ms. Taylor shook her head, "I don't really know what is going to happen now. I promised Jen that I wouldn't tell the aunt about the affair between Josie and the uncle. This thing is really a mess."

"He should damn well be arrested and charged," Richard sounded savage. He wiped a hand across his face. "Listen I am going to get something to drink." With that he walked out of the room.

As soon as he was gone Rita turned to her mother. "Did Jen tell you that she and Richard are serious about seeing each other?"

"No. No, she didn't. She didn't mention him." Ms. Taylor made a sound of distress. "Are you sure that they are serious, Rita? You know how Richard is."

"I didn't know how serious it was until he told me just now,"

"Well, that explains it his attitude now," her mother mused. "Although even if he wasn't serious about her, he would feel uncomfortable living here with her."

"If he was serious about her, what is he going to do now?"

Ms. Taylor stood up. "I think that is something that Richard and Jen will have to work out by themselves. It is a messy business and I wish I could have convinced Jen to press charges against that man for what he did to her. Maybe I will get somewhere with the aunt. I hope so. I will also try talking to Josie. In the meantime," she looked warningly at Rita, "do not interfere. Let Richard and Jen solve their own problems. Okay?"

"Okay, Mom. I will leave them strictly alone."

"Good. Let me go and see if I can get some more sleep." She too left the room.

Rita decided to check up on Richard.

He was in the kitchen, leaning against the window and staring out. He was drinking.

Rita sniffed the air, "Richard, remember that you have to be sober tomorrow to face the aunt and uncle."

"Do me a favor and go to bed." He did not turn around, neither did he look up.

Rita stood at the kitchen door for a minute, undecided. Richard's face hardened and his look did not encourage any further comment. For once Rita decided to leave it alone. Shrugging, she went back into the dining room and got out the folding bed. This she set up in a corner of the dining room, to the back wall. She went back into Richard's room for a pillow and two sheets, one to sleep on and the other to use as a cover. Back in the dining room she made up the bed and settled in. Richard was still in the kitchen when she fell asleep.

Chapter 16

The Taylors were all up early the following morning. Rita and her mother were fixing breakfast when Richard entered the kitchen.

"Where is Jen?" he asked, looking around.

"Still in the bedroom," his mother answered.

Rita looked carefully at him. His eyes looked a bit bloodshot, but he seemed okay.

"Is she planning to spend the whole day there?"

"Give her time Richard. You can't expect her to forget what happened in just one night. You are going to have to give her time to adjust," Ms. Taylor had also noted Richard's bloodshot eyes, but she did not comment.

Richard turned away, "I suppose Rita told you that I was serious with her."

"Was?"

"I don't know what to do. I can't just forget that this happened and continue on just as before."

"You men!" Rita banged a pot down in the counter. "What do you imagine the poor girl is thinking? You should be comforting her now, instead you're backing off."

"Will you get off my case! You don't know a thing about this." Richard had turned around, although he sounded angry, there was an element of confused frustration in his voice.

"I know enough to know that you aren't treating her right. I know how I would feel if I had been raped."

"I don't believe this! Dear sweet Jesus, Mom,"

Richard appealed to his mother, wiping his hand down his face, "Here I was trying to go easy with the girl and she allowed that rutting old man to rape her."

"There is no such thing as 'allowing someone to rape you", his mother calmly pointed out.

He swore.

"Richard!"

He turned away again. "Sorry," he muttered.

"Do you know what his problem is Mom?" Rita inserted, "He wanted to be the first with her and now he feels that she has been used. It's ..."

"No! " Richard objected violently, turning to face her, "That's not true."

"Shh... This argument is getting us nowhere, besides Jen may hear you if you don't lower your voice." As Rita opened her mouth to add something else, her mother raised her hands. "I said that's enough Rita. I warned you last night that this is something that Richard and Jen will have to deal with on their own. Richard," she added turning to him, "Can you be ready in half an hour. Jen's uncle leaves for work at eight and I want to catch him before he leaves."

Richard nodded once, "I'll be ready."

At the look in her son's eyes his mother warned, "Please Richard. No fighting. This is a serious matter and picking a fight with the man will only make matter's worse, besides I don't want to see you beaten up or arrested."

"He won't beat me up."

"Richard," she pleaded.

Rubbing the back of his neck, Richard turned to stare out the kitchen window, he sighed, "Mom," he said quietly, "There is no way I can go to that house and not punch that man."

Rita silently agreed.

Recognizing the finality of her son's tone, Ms. Taylor shook her head as she imagined the scene to come. "Oh dear," she said.

Now Richard looked slightly amused. He came over to pat his mother lightly on her shoulder, "Don't worry Mom. He sounds like the type who will curl up at the first punch."

"Just be careful," she begged.

"And you had better not go and underestimate him," Rita warned, she turned to her mother, "Do you want me to call Jason, Mom?"

Ms. Taylor shook her head, "No. The aunt should be home by nine so hopefully things won't be too bad."

Rita accompanied them, and the three arrived at Jen's home shortly before eight. They walked up the driveway and knocked on the door.

Inside Jack was no way near ready. He had got up at his usual time of seven o'clock and had taken a shower. Jen and Josie usually took turns fixing breakfast in the morning. When he saw neither one, he simply figured that Jen might not want to face him this morning. He wrapped himself in his toweling robe and went across to Josie's room. Her door was locked, which was unusual.

"Josie!" he called, "Josie!" He rapped sharply on the door.

After repeated calls and raps, Josie at last responded.

"I'm coming. I'm coming."

She opened the door to a furious Jack. "Why the locked door?" he asked rattling the knob.

She looked sulky.

Jack decided to leave it. It was getting late, and he wanted his breakfast. "Look, will you just fix something for me? Make it something simple since it's so late."

"Jen is supposed to fix breakfast today," Josie grumbled.

"I don't see Jen and I'm not in the mood for an argument right now. Just fix the breakfast and you can go back to bed." He turned and walked off.

"Beast," Josie muttered at his back. She walked over to Jen's room passing the open door of the bathroom. Jen's room door was slightly ajar, and she was about to knock when she noted a sheet on the floor of the empty bathroom. Josie looked around, puzzled. Jen was ridiculously tidy. Why would she leave a sheet on the bathroom floor? Josie went in and picked it up. Her heart skipped a beat then speeded up when she saw the dried blood. She took the sheet with her back into Jen's room without knocking. The first thing she saw was Jen's night dress on the floor.

"Oh, my God! Oh, my God!"

Frowning, she entered the room, bent and picked up the clothing. It was badly ripped and not far away Jen's panties were lying, also ripped. She held them up in both hands. Her heart began thumping faster. She then noticed the disordered and sheetless bed. She dropped the things and backed out of the room. What had happened? Jen was not in the house. She was sure of that, but where was she? She went back into her room and locked the door. Her hands were trembling. Something awful had happened. Was Jen dead? Did Jack know anything? He couldn't have killed her, could he? But then, where was she? Josie began to cry. She had no idea what to do or where to go. She was still standing in her room crying when Jack banged on her door.

"Josie! Where's the breakfast I asked you to make?"

Josie sniffed. She began backing away from the door, then remembering that her other door opened onto the verandah, she turned running toward the door.

"Josie! What's going on? Why do you keep locking the door?" Jack was banging on the door again.

Josie did not answer. She was about to open the door to the veranda when she heard a knocking on the front door. Without thinking, or finding out who it was, she opened her door. The only person of the trio she recognized was Rita. She had never met Ms. Taylor or Richard.

"Good morning Josie. I am Ms. Taylor, Rita's mother," Ms. Taylor greeted her. "Is something wrong?" she added. Josie did not immediately respond. She just stood there looking scared, and she had opened the door dressed only in a scanty nightie.

"I don't know where Jen is," Josie blurted out tearfully.

"She's at our house," Rita informed her.

Josie did not get a chance to respond. Jack, on hearing the voices had gone around, and now opened the main front door.

"Who are these people Josie?" he demanded. "What do they want?"

"I'm Ms. Taylor," Ms. Taylor repeated, before Josie could reply. "I'm here to see a Mr. Ferris."

"Jen is at your house?" Josie had finally found her voice. "Is she all right?"

"What is this about? What do you mean Jen's at

your house?" he sounded distinctly hostile.

"Are you Mr. Ferris?" Richard inquired, mildly.

"What if I am?"

"A Jack Ferris raped Jen early this morning..." Richard began.

"That's a lie," Jack shouted.

"Let's go inside," Ms. Taylor urged, "We don't want the entire neighborhood to know our business."

Jack recognized the sense of this. He backed in the living room, allowing them to follow him. "If she told you that I raped her, she is lying. The little slut! I may have been a little rough with her, but I sure didn't rape her. I've been sleeping with both of them." he boasted, "They practically begged me to. Ask her sister."

At that Richard saw red. Taking a step forward, he swung a solid right. His fist connected with a thud on the older man's undefended left jaw. Jack stumbled, then took two quick steps backwards as he tried to regain his balance. His arms flayed out as his knees collided with the center table. He went crashing down on the table, knocking the vase of flowers flying. Still unable to regain his balance, his momentum carried him over and off the low table, where he crashed into the wall.

Josie's had her hand over her mouth which had opened in a silent ~O~.

Rita had grabbed her mother and both of them huddled together, slightly to the left of Josie. Richard was rubbing his knuckles. He looked satisfied.

Jack got awkwardly to his feet. There was an ugly look on his face. He didn't even notice that he had cut his hand on a splinter of glass. Swearing he rounded the table and charged at Richard without pausing. That was his undoing. Richard was ready for him. He ducked Jack's first punch, which landed harmlessly on his shoulder, then released another one of his own, this time to the solar plexus. As Jack doubled over Richard brought his knee up striking directly at the other man's groin.

"Ahhh..." Jack moaned as he folded onto the floor, both hands clutching at his privates.

Richard called him something unprintable.

Jack remained where he had fallen. He was still moaning as Richard moved towards him.

"No, Richard, no!" Ms. Taylor called out. She detangled herself from Rita and hurried across to her son. She grabbed him about his middle to prevent him from going after Jack again. "That's enough. He is hurt."

Richard was actually trembling with the force of his emotions. He did not try to break away from his mother, instead he hugged her, his head resting on her shoulder. After a while he raised is head muttering, "Let's get Jen's things."

His mother nodded.

Josie, her hand still over her mouth whispered, "Is Jen all right?"

Ms. Taylor turned to her, smiling in reassurance, "I'm sure she will be. I am going to take her to the doctor today. Where's her room?"

Josie led the way. Jack was still moaning on the ground.

Once in Jen's bedroom, Ms. Taylor and Rita did not comment on the sheets or ripped night gown. Ms. Taylor turned to Josie, "We only want to take enough things for a week. We haven't got any boxes or a car so we can't take much today. Will you help Rita to pack up what's needed?"

Josie nodded, "Is Jen going to stay with you?" She did not wait for an answer. "Can I come too? It won't take me long to pack. I don't want to stay here with Jack now."

Ms. Taylor could hardly refuse. "Of course, Josie," she said.

Josie turned to Rita, "I'll take her things out and give you a bag then you can pack while I get my things. Okay?"

"Okay," Rita agreed.

The moaning in the living room stopped. Richard turned to go back out. His mother held his arm, "Please Richard. No more."

"I won't hit him again. I just want to see what he's doing."

She freed his arm but followed him.

Jack was slowly heading for the master bedroom. He was still bent over, and there was a grimace of pain on his face.

"Oh dear," Ms. Taylor worried; "I hope he isn't seriously hurt."

"I hope he is," Richard was unmoved by the man's obvious pain. "If you're thinking of calling the police," he called across to Jack, "Don't forget that my mother is taking Jen to the doctor today. We plan on getting documented proof that she was raped."

Jack did not answer.

Richard and his mother watched as he disappeared into the opposite wing of the house.

"I doubt that he will be doing anything in the near future." Richard commented with satisfaction.

"Let's just hope he doesn't call the police."

"He won't," Richard was confident. "He is too

scared. Right now, he doesn't know that Jen isn't going to report what happened." He turned away, "Let's help Rita so that we can get out of here."

They were still there when Aunt Beryl arrived. She arrived shortly before nine to find her front doors open.

"Hello?" she called on entering. "Josie? Jen? Why are the doors open? Who broke the vase?"

Ms. Taylor came out of Josie's bedroom where she had been supervising the packing.

"Hello. I am Ms. Taylor," she stretched out her hand as she approached Josie's aunt.

Aunt Beryl shook her hand cautiously. "Where is everybody? Is there something wrong?" she asked.

"There certainly is," Ms. Taylor pronounced, "Will you sit down while I try to explain?"

Mystified, Aunt Beryl sank down on one of the settees.

Bluntly, Ms. Taylor told her exactly what had occurred, "Jen came to our house, terrified, this morning. Your husband had raped her. She..."

Aunt Beryl didn't give her a chance to continue. She jumped up, "This is ridiculous! How dare you accuse my husband of such a thing?"

"He is in your bedroom if you care to ask him." Richard had stood listening by the corridor to the bathroom.

"And Jen's ripped up clothing and the sheets are still in the bedroom," Rita inserted. "Covered in blood!"

Aunt Beryl hadn't noticed them before. "Who are you?" she demanded.

"I am Richard Taylor, and this is my sister Rita."

"Oh! So, you are the man that Jen was carrying on with. How dare you come into my house with these ridiculous accusations? What have you done? Got her pregnant? Let me warn you that ..."

"Beryl!" it was Jack, he had obviously heard the altercation and come to investigate. "Don't listen to them I can explain everything. I didn't rape anybody."

"She was raped!" Richard bit out.

"She damn well begged me to take her!" Jack retorted. He turned to his wife again, "Why would I need to rape anyone. Listen, you call Josie in here. Ask her if she didn't beg me to make love to her. You ask her."

"Only because you said that you loved me. You told me that you were going to divorce Aunt Beryl," Josie had quietly entered the room and was now standing by Richard's side.

Aunt Beryl had had enough. "You two-faced bitch," she screamed, pointing an accusing finger at Josie. "I want you out of my house. I don't believe this." She held her head in both hands. Jack started towards her. "Get away from me! Get away from me! Oh my God. I don't believe this! I just want you all out. You Josie, you're an ungrateful piece of trash. After I took you in and cared for you when your parents died. This is the thanks I get." she raised her voice again, "Just get out of my house! Now!"

Josie turned away in embarrassment. She did not look at Jack, who was almost wringing his hands.

Ms. Taylor felt it time to intervene, "Both girls will be staying with me Mrs. Ferris, but they will need funds to survive. I understand there was a trust set up by their parents?"

"Don't worry. I don't want their money. I wash my hands of the both of them. I will give you the lawyers name and they can look after things for themselves from now on;

or you can. I don't care." She dug into her bag for the necessary information, muttering imprecations under her breath at the same time.

In the meanwhile, Richard began helping Rita to move two suitcases and a bag onto the verandah.

Aunt Beryl finally handed Ms. Taylor a slip of paper with the lawyer's name on it. She watched with indifference as the suitcases were moved out. "The only thing in here that belongs to them is their clothes. Nothing else. I bought every stick of furniture in their room with my own money."

"Don't worry we are only taking clothing," Ms. Taylor assured her. "We will have to come back for the rest of their thing,"

"Well, you'd better do so by Friday. After that I am throwing everything out."

It was with relief that Ms. Taylor left the house. Both Josie and Rita were silent on the walk home. Josie was practically in tears. Richard made occasional derogatory comments about the Ferrises. Ms. Taylor had to agree with him. It was bad enough what Jack had done, but the aunt had compounded the wrong. She wondered what tall tale he was now telling his wife, and whether she would believe him. She would have been pleasantly taken aback at the scene that followed after they left the house.

Aunt Beryl and Jack had watched in silence as the Taylors and Josie left. As the doors closed behind than Jack spoke up, "Well that is that. I'm sorry Beryl, but you don't know the hell that those two put me through."

"They put you through!" Aunt Beryl gave a bitter

laugh. "I'm going to see my lawyer today. In the meantime, I am moving my things to this side of the house." She pointed to Josie's and Jen's rooms.

"Come on Beryl, surely you don't believe them?"

"I believe that you slept with them, and they are my flesh and blood even though they have turned out to be little better than sluts. Well, you can have them. But not here; not under my roof or in my bed. Besides which, I think that I've put up with enough of your so-called lovemaking. The twins might want you. I don't."

"You bitch," Jack was furious. "And then you wonder why I have to turn to other women."

Aunt Beryl backed away on seeing the violent mood he was in. Even so she was warning as she moved, "Don't you dare touch me. You lay a single hand on me and I'm calling the police. I'll also back up Jen's story."

"Okay, move to the other side of the house, see if I care." Jack taunted as he turned to walk back to their bedroom, "But just remember that this house is in both our names. You'll be living here for some time. I'm not selling, and you can't without my signature on the papers."

Aunt Beryl said nothing. She was confident that her lawyers would be able to arrange something.

Chapter 17

Four weeks later Ms. Taylor was still trying to get Jen to socialize more. She had insisted that Jen see a doctor right after the incident and in an effort to avoid any possibility of pregnancy the gynecologist had recommended a dilatation and curettage. However, apart from the follow-up visits to the doctor and a few shopping trips Jen had stayed home. Unfortunately, both she and Josie missed their final Physics exam. Monique and Rita had tried getting Jen out of the house more but to no avail. Jen refused to go on the trip to the Cayman Islands and even refused to speak to Richard. She had insisted however that the others not cancel the trip. In the end Richard did not go. Monique and Rita went with their boyfriends. However, according to Rita the trip was a disaster. Since their return a few days ago from what Ms. Taylor had learned Rita and Monique were no longer talking to each other and both girls and broken off with their boyfriends.

She was busy in the kitchen, kneading the floor to make dumpling for the soup pot, when she looked out the window and saw Richard. He had obviously been waiting for her to acknowledge him. Once she had, he started a series of pantomime gestures. Ms. Taylor guessed that he wanted to come in but decided to ignore him for a while. He was her son, but she was a little disappointed in his behavior so far.

The day after Jen and Josie had moved in Richard had moved out. Since then, he had returned occasionally, but only to collect his things or to see his mother or sister. He did not ask to see Jen and Jen of course was avoiding him. That Ms. Taylor could understand. What she couldn't accept was Richard's ready acceptance of her refusal. Despite telling Rita not to interfere she had tried talking to Jen, but Jen refused to discuss Richard. Jen it seemed was just too embarrassed and wanted to simply forget to whole thing. Ms. Taylor suspected that if she could, Jen would have preferred to live elsewhere, and would have blanked out anyone and anything even remotely connected to her past from her memory. In that respect, she was glad that for now Jen was being forced to confront and deal with the reality of her situation.

Richard's problem was that he couldn't forget what had happened. In her talks with him, Ms. Taylor sensed that although he still cared for Jen, he felt somehow betrayed. He felt that Jen could have prevented her rape; that she should have confided in him from the beginning or should have been more suspicious of her uncle. Although he had not gone so far as to repeat that Jen had actually invited her rape, he had come pretty close, in an argument that had left a bitter taste in both their mouths. It brought her close to wishing that she had never got involved in the twin's problems. Worse was what he had suggested. That she was attacking his position simply because he was a man and since the break-up with their father, she had a thing against all men.

Regrettably, she could not operate as juvenile as her children were acting. She now bent over the sink to dust off her hands and moved to open the back door.

"Is Jen here?" Richard asked as he stepped in, looking about as if expecting to see her pop up at any time.

"Why? Do you actually want to see her or are you asking just so you can avoid bumping into her?"

"I want to see her," he muttered. Richard shuffled his feet in embarrassment as his mother stared at him. "I want to apologize for my behavior so far."

His mother was amazed. She folded her arms across her bosom, opened her mouth to say something, then decided that her best move at this point would probably be to keep quiet.

"Oh," was all she ended up saying.

Richard cleared his throat, "So is she here?"

"Yes." Then, "Oh no!" Ms. Taylor brought a hand to her forehead as she remembered something, "Have you heard what has happened?"

"About Josie?" Richard was nodding, "Rita came and told me yesterday. I didn't even know that she lost the baby."

Ms. Taylor hesitated, thinking aloud, "I had better tell her you're here."

"No. Don't Mom," Richard took a quick step forward. "You know that she will just say she won't see me."

His mother was still hesitant. "Do you think that it's a good idea to see her now?"

"Come on, Mom. This is what you have been begging me to do."

"I know," Ms. Taylor agreed quietly, "but I want to be sure that it is what you want to do, especially now."

Richard came up and hugged his mother. "It is Mom. I like her mom. I… I do want to be with her. I just…" he sighed. "After Rita left last night, I spent some time thinking about the whole thing. I've really been selfish, and I think it is about time I stared making amends."

His mother smile, "Okay, she is in your bed-room."

Richard left his mother and went over to his old bedroom. He knocked once on the door.

"Who is it?"

Instead of answering he knocked again.

"Who is it?

Richard turned the knob. "I'm coming in," he announced.

"Richard?"

He entered as soon as he heard Jen's enquiry.

"Richard!" she exclaimed again as he entered. She had been standing looking out the window, doing nothing as far as Richard could make out.

"Hi." As he came towards her, Jen turned her face away. Richard came and stood directly in front of her. "I only just heard about Josie. I'm sorry."

Jen gave him a quick glance then looked down at her hand loosely clasped together.

Josie had taken Jack's betrayal hard and after moving to the Taylor's, more and more she seemed to take on Jen's former personality. The difference being she didn't even want to speak to Jen. For the entire time she had been at the Taylors she had barely spoken a work. Jen became so worried about her that Ms. Taylor finally agreed something was wrong and insisted that Josie see a regular doctor, since the midwife at the clinic where she was been seen consistently shrugged off her depression as "normal for a single teenage mother." Josie was subsequently admitted to Kingston Public Hospital for psychiatric evaluation.

She did not stay there long. Four days after being admitted she simply wandered out of the hospital. She had obviously planned to walk it home as she didn't have any money for the bus fare. She didn't make it, however. She was hit by a car as she crossed the street, just a few blocks from the hospital. Although she escaped with only a mild concussion, she lost the baby.

That was the final straw. For the past few weeks, the baby had been the only thing that had sparked her interest. Word had soon spread in the community and at the school about her pregnancy. Even more so than Jen, she had virtually made the house her prison, leaving only to go to the clinic for her check- ups. She had refused to sit her final physics exam although the principal had okayed it. With the loss of the baby, it seemed that she had lost her last feeble attempt to maintain her grasp on reality. She was treated and released from the hospital the day after her accident; two days later she was again readmitted to the psychiatry ward of the hospital in a state of severe depression. That was yesterday.

"Listen Jen," Richard began, taking her hands.

Jen dragged her hands away, "I don't want your pity." She abruptly turned away from him and went back to staring out the window. "You don't need to apologize. Josie is not your concern. You can leave now."

Richard move closer, "Who says I pity you?"

Jen remained stubbornly silent. She folded her arms across her chest.

"I came to apologize for my behavior," Richard began again. "I'm sorry I've been such a jerk, about well... about what happened."

He stopped and ran a hand across the back of his

neck. "I guess I couldn't handle it and I sort of blamed you."

She did not respond.

"Jen?"

Her only response was to hug herself tighter and bend her head. At that he went over and hugged her from behind.

"Jen, I'm sorry," he repeated. "I'm sorry. I want us to be together. I'm hurting too but I know I didn't handle it well."

Jen turned in his arms and buried her head in his chest. She began to cry, "I can't cope with anything right now."

"Shhh… That's alright. I know I've been a jerk. Just don't block me out. We'll deal…take it as slow as you want. Just don't block me out."

Jen took some big breaths. "I feel it's my fault Josie's so depressed. I was so caught up in my problems that I didn't even think about her. She has always been the strong one and now the first time she really needed me I let her down."

"Shhh... That's not true," he patted her gently. "If you hadn't been so eager to stand by her all these months, you would never have been in the situation to get …." He stopped abruptly.

"Raped," Jen completed baldly.

"Yes," he said seriously. "I can deal with it Jen. But you can't blame yourself for that… or Josie's problem now."

Jen did not respond.

"Jen, I …I've been a fool only thinking about myself. You have been the opposite."

"What do you mean?"

"You've been trying every which way to help your twin instead of thinking about yourself. You pressured Mom in to getting her help. None of us realized she was getting so depressed."

"It's not just that."

"Then explain."

"You don't understand," Jen wailed.

When she only sniffed, he persisted, "Come on Jen, there's been enough misunderstanding between us."

"I became totally dependent on Josie after our parents died. I wanted to be dependent on her. It never occurred to me and certainly not to her that I was leaning on her too much. It was only after I found out about her and Jack that I changed and decided to stand on my own two feet. I just feel that if I hadn't been so dependent on her she would never have needed Jack's love, and he would never have been able to fool her."

"I don't think so," Richard disagreed. "You told me that she wanted to manage you. You gave her that. It could be that it was her coping crutch. So, she was using you as much as you were using her.

Another thing, Josie was a fairly popular girl. It's not as if she didn't have any boyfriends. I think that it's just unfortunate that she fell in love with the wrong person, someone who abused her love and used her. The reason she became so depressed is not because she wanted to talk to you, and you weren't available. She became depressed because Jack did not love her, and she lost Jack's baby. You must have realized that. When she was here, she was totally preoccupied with that baby simply because it was Jack's baby."

Richard stopped to squeeze Jen's shoulders lightly, "You know that I'm right Jen." He did not add that he thought that her twin was particular selfish. From what he had heard he was sure that she had been aware of Jack's interest in Jen but had chosen not to convey her fears to Jen.

"I suppose so," Jen, while not fully in agreement, reluctantly nodded.

"Good. So, do you want to go out to the theatre tonight?"

"Tonight?"

"Why not?"

"But... I mean... You mean you still want to go out with me?"

"Would I be asking you out to the theatre if I didn't want to go out with you?"

Jen licked her lips nervously. "What are people saying?"

"You will have to come out to know."

Jen was still hesitant. "Are you sure, Richard? I can't…I don't…"

"I'm sure I want to go to the theatre with you."
Jen smiled shyly.
Richard grinned, then hugged her tightly.

Epilogue
One year later

Although Jen never took her final physics exam, She and Monique had gone on to the university together, both to the Faculty of Natural Science. Monique had planned on getting a degree in Zoology, while Jen was studying Computer Science. It was there that Monique met her present boyfriend and soon to be husband. Yes. Monique was getting married. Jen was going to be the maid of honor.

For the life of her, Jen couldn't fathom what Monique saw in the guy. He wasn't even good looking. He was dropping out of the university and had encouraged Monique to do the same. They planned on opening a bakery together—with the money Monique's mother had promised to give her as a wedding gift. Why a bakery? She was still waiting on the answer to that question.

She sometimes wondered whether Monique wasn't just trying to get back at her father. He didn't approve of this guy either; neither did Monique's aunt or uncle. And Monique's mother didn't seem to care. Jen had tried talking to Monique, but to no avail: She loved Ricky—the husband to be—and Ricky loved her, and that was that. Richard suggested that perhaps in choosing someone who wasn't good looking and who looked as if he might become financially dependent on her, Monique might just be trying to ensure that she had some kind of a hold over the guy, and he would then be unlikely to stray. Jen finally took Richard's advice. She decided to leave them alone.

Rita was still free, single and disengaged. She had moved on from Jason and was now seeing someone called Danny. She was also working as a secretary in the same government Ministry as her mother.

As far as Jen knew, her aunt and uncle were still living in the same house. They had not yet divorced but the marriage was just about dead. The house had been virtually divided in half, with her uncle and his girlfriend in one half and her aunt and a series of live-in lovers in the other. Jen suspected that there was an undeclared competition doing on. She was not particularly interested. She had seen neither of them since leaving and wanted to maintain the status quo. What information she had received about them, she had heard though the "grape-vine."

Josie was now doing fine. Two months after being admitted to the hospital she was released. Although she was no longer depressed, she was not the same outgoing person. With Ms. Taylor's help she was able to get a job in an office in New Kingston, since, for the time being, she was not capable of studying further.

Shortly after Josie's release from the hospital Jen decided that it was time that she and Josie moved out of the Taylor's house. She felt that Josie would recover faster if she moved completely out of the neighborhood and besides the house was too small to hold them all. Ms. Taylor adamantly opposed the idea. She was afraid that if the twins were living together, they would become too dependent on each other once again, perhaps setting themselves up for another tragedy. After much consultation with the doctors who were treating Josie, Jen was persuaded that it would be in Josie's best interest for the twins to live apart for now. Ms. Taylor's cousin took Josie in as a boarder and Jen found a room in Mona Heights; a community close to the university. She lived there until moving onto campus housing.

After an up and down beginning, Jen hadn't really expected her relationship with Richard to go anywhere. They were still seeing each other however. Jen knew that Richard had hopes of leaving Jamaica soon and that he wanted to study law. What would happen then she had no idea. She loved Richard and he seemed equally committed to her. She refused to worry too much about it. They had both decided to finish their studies before finalizing their relationship. Richard had been infinitely patient and kind, both in understanding her fears and giving her time to heal—mentally.

She was young, she was healthy, and she was unbelievable happy with her life.

Authors' Note:

She Likes Sugar is set in Jamaica, West Indies in the 1980s. Some descriptions are definitely from the past and no longer exist in current day Jamaica.

Explanations:

- In the early 1980s, grade school children at age 10 or 11 would sit the Common Entrance Examination. A pass meant a full tuition paid scholarship to high school, while a ½ pass meant a half scholarship.
- High schools used the term *form* instead of *grade*. Students started 1st form in high school at 11 or 12 and could graduate at 5th form.
- Students took the Ordinary "O" Level examination at the end of 5th form and could then enter college based on their "O" Level achievement. However, many students would elect to complete two additional years of 6th form–Lower and Upper six. This was the equivalent of an Advanced Placement or the 1st year in a college/university if, on completing 6th form, the student obtained a pass in their Advanced "A" Level examination.
- In "A" Level, the General Paper was similar to English.
- The Common Entrance Examination and the 'O" & "A" Level examinations were replaced by the Caribbean Examinations Council (**CXC**) in 1979.

- Other flashbacks include places, structures and events. Some examples are Ring Ding, the television program featuring Ms. Lou which stopped in 1980; public transportation provide by the Jamaica Omnibus Service (JOS), stopped in 1983; and Coconut Park, an amusement park adjacent to Hope Gardens closed in 1997.

Lyrics of Brown Girl in the Ring

"Brown Girl in the Ring" is a traditional children's song in the West Indies and was a favorite in Jamaica. It is often sung during ring games, and some have suggested it is a precursor to adult courtship. During the game the children form a circle by holding hands. One child skip to the center of the circle. The other in the circle then begins the questions. "Show me your motion." At this point the child in the center does his or her favorite dance. If asked "Show me your partner," he or she picks a friend to join him or her in the circle.

Brown girl in the ring
Tra la la la la
There's a brown girl in the ring
Tra la la la la la
Brown girl in the ring
Tra la la la la
She looks like a sugar in a plum
Plum plum

Show me your motion

She Likes Sugar

Tra la la la la
Come on show me your motion
Tra la la la la la
Show me your motion
Tra la la la la
She looks like a sugar in a plum
Plum plum

All had water run dry
Got nowhere to wash my cloths
All had water run dry
Got nowhere to wash my cloths

I remember one Saturday night
We had fried fish and Johnny-cakes
I remember one Saturday night
We had fried fish and Johnny-cakes

Beng-a-deng

Thank you for reading!

She Likes Sugar

by Jo Dinage

Author's Bio

Jo Dinage describes herself as a people watcher and enjoys trying to figure out what motivates others. She is the author of 5 young adult novels.

http://www.opeart.com by mailto:olive@opeart.com

www.ingramcontent.com/pod-product-compliance
Lightning Source LLC
Chambersburg PA
CBHW020800190726
48285CB00006B/2110